THE DEVIL'S MARSHAL

When Lucinda Latimer is accused of murdering Archibald Harper, her bounty hunter brother Brodie is convinced of her innocence. Vowing to find the culprit, he turns up a witness in the form of drunken varmint Wilfred Clay — who, minutes after admitting to seeing the real killer, is shot to death on his own front porch. All the clues point to the murderer being Derrick Shelby — the man known as 'the devil's marshal'. The only trouble is, Derrick died a year ago . . .

I. J. PARNHAM

THE DEVIL'S MARSHAL

Complete and Unabridged

LINFORD
Leicester

First published in Great Britain in 2013 by
Robert Hale Limited
London

First Linford Edition
published 2015
by arrangement with
Robert Hale Limited
London

A catalogue record for this book is available
from the British Library.

ISBN 978–1–4448–2646–3

Published by
F. A. Thorpe (Publishing)
Anstey, Leicestershire

Set by Words & Graphics Ltd.
Anstey, Leicestershire
Printed and bound in Great Britain by
T. J. International Ltd., Padstow, Cornwall

This book is printed on acid-free paper

1

'I need a room for a few days,' Brodie Latimer said. 'I don't know how long for yet.'

'Take your pick of the rooms and stay for as long as you like,' Genevieve Shelby, the black-clad hotel owner, said with a thin smile. 'Nobody else is staying here.'

Her reply made Brodie frown. Hamilton was busy, the Shelby Hotel was clean and located in the centre of town, and the rates were reasonable, but he didn't question his luck as he signed his name in the indicated space.

He wasn't surprised when his name made Genevieve flinch before she reassumed her good host demeanour and directed him to follow her up the stairs. She picked a large room that looked across the main drag at the law office and courtroom.

After she'd indicated the view, she met his eye, but he ignored the opportunity to explain his reason for coming to Hamilton and instead complimented her choice of room. When she left, he considered the scene outside, which, while he'd been booking the room, had developed into a worrying one.

Earlier, when he'd spoken with Marshal Kyle Duffield, people had begun to gather outside the law office. Now their numbers had swelled so that the crowd blocked half of the road and this critical mass of people had created a disruption that was encouraging more people to join them.

Kyle had promised him that he could return at sundown. That was an hour away, but with the crowd growing in size and rowdiness by the minute, it felt unlikely that the lawman would be able to honour his promise.

He still headed outside where he skirted around the crowd and went in search of a quiet saloon. He could fulfil only half of his requirements as the two saloons in town were both bustling.

In the Sundown saloon, customers were jostling each other at the windows as they watched the people gather. So he went to the Four Aces saloon around the corner, which didn't have a view of that part of town. Even so, the events there were the only topic of conversation.

'They're sure to find her guilty tomorrow.'

'They should hang her tonight and get this over with quickly.'

'Hanging is too good for a woman who did what she did.'

Brodie overheard these views and others that were equally one-sided before he reached the bar. When he had a whiskey in hand, he joined one of the many opinionated groups where he nodded at the appropriate times while listening for any information that would give him hope.

Tomorrow morning Lucinda Latimer, his younger sister, was to be tried for murdering Archibald Harper.

As youngsters, Lucinda had been restless and unwilling to accept a life of toil in the small settlement of Dirtwood. She'd always been in trouble while Brodie had spent his time sorting out trouble.

Accordingly, as young adults, while Lucinda had run away with unspecified plans to seek a better life, Brodie had accepted an appointment as a deputy to the town's first marshal. Before long, the meagre rewards had encouraged him to leave town and become a manhunter instead.

Over the last seven years, he'd built a reputation as a bounty hunter who always found his quarry. He'd often wondered about Lucinda's fate, although he hadn't thought she'd commit a serious crime.

So when he'd read in a newspaper that she'd been accused of murder, he'd been shocked. As Lucinda was the only family he had left, he'd abandoned his hunt for the outlaw Phineas Moon and had headed north to Hamilton.

Sadly, if the gossip he'd heard was right, she would be found guilty.

When the low sun edged into view and cast its dying rays across the saloon room, Brodie moved to slip away. That had the unfortunate effect of drawing attention to him for the first time.

'I don't know you,' the nearest drinker said. 'What are you here for?'

When Brodie had ridden into town, he'd resolved not to hide his identity, but what he'd seen and heard since had convinced him that discretion would be more sensible.

'Nothing much,' Brodie said after struggling to come up with a suitable answer.

'I saw you earlier,' another man said, 'heading into the law office. Are you here for the trial?'

'I'm just here,' Brodie said with a warm smile, 'for a short while.'

He moved towards the door, but he hadn't soothed his questioners' concerns as consternation broke out behind him. He chided himself for failing to provide better answers, as clearly the townsfolk were eager for gossip about the trial and even the hint that someone might know something had excited this group.

So when he reached the door a line of men trailed behind him shouting out for him to stop. He slipped outside, took a smart left, and headed down the road, an action that enflamed his eager followers even more as they hurried out after him.

By the time he reached the corner of the road, his small hope that he could make his appointment without fuss died. Ahead, the crowd had grown to an unruly mob of around a hundred people.

Torches were being lit and excited chatter filled the evening. Brodie glanced over his shoulder and that made his followers gesture and shout at him, so Brodie hurried into the crowd.

Within moments people surrounded him, but they were stationary and so he was able to wend his way towards the law office without difficulty. Unfortunately, this meant his pursuers were also able to move quickly through the mob.

He'd covered only a quarter of the way to the law office when he and his unwanted retinue gathered the interest of those ahead. He avoided catching anyone's eye and slipped past another five people until someone blocked his path.

He moved to the left, but the man moved that way, too, and so he darted to the right, an action that encouraged others to join in and form a barrier. Then a hand clamped down on his shoulder and dragged him round.

'What you got to hide?' the red-faced and liquor-fuelled man demanded.

'Nothing,' Brodie said. 'I've got business in the law office.'

'What business?'

Brodie didn't have an answer and so he tried to back away, but the mob had closed in; by now, everyone was watching the altercation eagerly.

'He went into the law office earlier,' one man said.

'And he's only just arrived in town,' another man said.

'I saw him go in to the Shelby Hotel,' a third man offered.

In an instant, the lively mood turned sour as this comment appeared to convince everyone his intentions were suspicious. Someone shoved him, knocking him into two other men, who took exception to being pushed and pushed back.

He fought to keep his balance and he accidentally barged someone over before he tripped over another man's foot. He crashed to the ground before rolling into a forest of legs.

He came to rest lying amidst people who wouldn't know why he'd been knocked over, but that didn't stop them kicking and prodding him. He reached to the ground to try to lever himself to his feet, but someone stood on his hand.

The wall of people pressed in around him and more kicks slammed into his side. Before he became trapped and someone did him serious damage, he hunched over and crawled his way along the ground.

He made more headway than he expected giving him the impression that people had backed away. He extended his neck, turtle-like, to see if he'd been reprieved, but that only let him see that one of his irate pursuers was standing over him.

This man dragged him to his feet and then drew back his fist as he aimed to punch him back down again. Brodie raised a fist, but he didn't need to defend himself as a gunshot sounded, making everyone freeze.

Marshal Kyle Duffield slipped through the suddenly still and quiet throng with Deputy Erskine Farlow at his shoulder. While Erskine glared at his assailant until he backed away, Kyle faced Brodie and jerked his thumb over his shoulder.

Brodie shot his assailant a warning glance that said the lawmen's intervention had saved only him from a beating before he turned away and walked down a passageway that had formed through the crowd. Everyone turned to watch his progress to the law office. When he reached it, he walked straight in, but the lawmen followed him only to the door.

'You've made your feelings clear, people,' Kyle shouted. 'Now go about your business. Lucinda Latimer will face an open trial tomorrow and justice will be done.'

His comment gathered a supportive cheer, but only from a portion of the crowd.

'What's that man doing here?' someone demanded to a louder chorus of approval.

'That's not your concern.' Kyle raised his voice when several men shouted that it was. 'But I'll make it my concern if you don't stop blocking the road.'

The two lawmen faced the mob and Brodie helped the situation by moving out of view. For a minute they stood silently and Brodie was wondering if a confrontation was inevitable when sense prevailed and people on the periphery peeled away.

For a few minutes Kyle watched the dispersal gather pace before he headed inside. When the deputy had closed the door, Kyle considered Brodie, his hands on his hips.

'Obliged you came when you did,' Brodie said. 'That was about to get messy.'

Kyle glanced through the window at the mob that was still moving away, although their angry muttering confirmed that more trouble was likely.

'It was,' he said with an exasperated sigh. 'You shouldn't have told anyone your name.'

'The trouble is, I didn't tell them who I am. They just took exception to me.'

Brodie smiled and Kyle took the

opportunity to lighten the mood with a laugh.

'You've got fifteen minutes. If the trial doesn't end tomorrow, you can return again tomorrow night.'

'You reckon it could be over with that quickly?'

Kyle signified for Erskine to unlock the door to the small jailhouse.

'She's not got a defence.'

With this grim assessment ringing in his ears Brodie took a deep breath and then headed into the jailhouse. Four cells were set together in the centre of a square room that had a bench around the walls.

There were three prisoners inside. Two men were in the far left cell and Lucinda was in the near right one.

This arrangement was presumably the safest for her, although her cropped hair and male attire could let her, under casual scrutiny, pass for being a man. The other prisoners were asleep, but Lucinda was sitting up on her cot with an ear raised high, presumably in concern about the developing situation outside.

Lucinda considered Brodie without interest until he sat down on the bench facing her and then looked up so that the shadows didn't hide his face. She flinched upright with sudden recognition and a wide smile appeared on her face.

'I didn't expect you,' she said with genuine relief in her tone.

'You couldn't expect me,' Brodie said. 'You didn't tell me you were in here.'

'I couldn't get in touch after seven years to tell you I was about to go to jail for murder, but I'm pleased you've come to see me as a free woman for one last time.' Lucinda rolled her legs off the cot and then considered him before shrugging. 'I'd heard you're now a manhunter.'

Brodie smiled, appreciating Lucinda's breezy method of dealing with this awkward encounter.

'I've taken the details of ten men and

I've collected ten bounties. I was looking for the eleventh when I heard about you.' Brodie rubbed his jaw as he struggled to think of anything else to say about his life before finishing lamely. 'What had you been doing, before all this happened?'

'I took work wherever I could find it.' Her eyes became troubled and so she glanced away and sighed, clearly unwilling to explain more. 'Then recently I got a decent job working in the Shelby Hotel. Genevieve didn't get many guests, but that was fine with me.'

They sat in silence for a while contemplating each other and this let Brodie hear a clock ticking in the main office, reminding him that he didn't have much longer.

'What happened between you and this Archibald Harper?'

'Nothing.'

'The man's dead and you must know something about the circumstances or you wouldn't be sitting there.'

'His killer must know something.'

14

She gave him a long stare. 'I don't.'

Brodie lowered his head and rubbed the back of his neck as he collected his thoughts. He had been sure Lucinda would be honest with him and he judged that her dismissive answer was a truthful one.

'So tell me what you do know.'

Lucinda got up and paced the cell twice before facing him.

'Archibald and I had been getting close. One night I invited him to come up to my room, but he and Genevieve had once argued and he was reluctant to come in. So I bade him goodnight. I never saw him again.' Lucinda sighed. 'Later his body was found lying in the old depot and as I was the last person to be seen with him, Marshal Duffield threw me in here.'

'That's a weak reason to think you guilty,' Brodie considered. 'Can anyone back up your story?'

'Wilfred Clay saw me go back into the hotel and he saw Archibald head out to the depot alone, but my lawyer says that won't help. Wilfred's a no-good varmint and the worst person to rely on for your defence.'

Brodie raised his voice as a key rattled in the jailhouse door.

'But if nobody else will speak up for you, this could end in only one way.'

'Which brings us back to where we started.' Lucinda leaned forward and looked him over intently, as if she were committing his image to memory. 'I'm pleased you came to see me for one last time.'

2

Wilfred Clay lived beyond the small, abandoned railroad depot to the north of Hamilton. Archibald's body had been found in one of the four gaunt timber warehouses, and Brodie dallied there for a while before moving on to Wilfred's house.

Even before he spoke with Wilfred, Brodie decided Lucinda had been right; Wilfred was the worst person to speak up in her defence.

His ramshackle house must have been well constructed many years ago, but now it stood at an angle with holes in the walls and roof. Only the rotting detritus of old farm implements that had been piled up against the walls appeared to be keeping the house from falling over.

The trial was due to start in an hour and it was only two hours after sunup,

17

but Wilfred was already lying sprawled out on the trash-strewn porch working his way through a bottle of whiskey.

'Is it time for me to go?' Wilfred slurred, looking up at him with rheumy and glazed eyes.

'I don't work for the court,' Brodie said. 'I'm Lucinda's brother.'

'I never knew she had no brother.' Wilfred wiped the top of the bottle on a ragged and grimy sleeve and held it out.

Brodie shook his head as he searched for a clean spot to sit amidst the rotting food and discarded bottles. When he couldn't find one, he located a rusty bucket and upturned it to sit on.

'But Lucinda told me about you. You're her only hope.'

Wilfred shivered and then sought solace in the bottle.

'I can't tell nobody nothing,' he said between gulps, 'about what she and Archibald did that night.'

'Nobody would expect you to. You can only tell the truth about what you saw.'

Wilfred gave a doubtful look. 'I told you. I don't know what happened that night. I don't know what happens most nights. They all run into one.'

Brodie reckoned that was an accurate account of Wilfred's life, but he was her only hope and so he held out a hand for the bottle. When Wilfred passed it over, he placed it on the porch between his feet and fixed Wilfred with his firm gaze.

'A decent woman is relying on you to speak up for her. You have an hour to sober up, get cleaned up, and get your thoughts in order.'

Wilfred cackled and, in a moment of self-awareness, gestured at his ragged and grime-encrusted clothing, indicating that even if he had a month, it wouldn't be long enough.

'Nobody wants to hear what old Wilfred Clay has got to say.' The laughter petered out and he tried to wrest the whiskey bottle back, but he struggled to raise himself and, eventually, flopped down on to his side. 'Even if someone did, they won't let me say it.'

Brodie had been shaking his head sadly, his misgivings about going to Wilfred's house growing, but the last comment piqued his interest. So he went over to Wilfred and dragged him up to a sitting position before leaning him back against the wall.

'What do you want to say?' he asked, hunkering down before him. 'And who will stop you saying it?'

'The truth, and them.'

Wilfred waved an arm, seemingly indicating the whole town, and that unbalanced him. He righted himself and offered Brodie a lopsided, gap-toothed grin.

When Wilfred said nothing else, Brodie collected the whiskey bottle and swirled the contents tantalizingly before Wilfred's face.

'Are you saying you know who killed Archibald Harper?'

Wilfred's eyes rocked from side to side as he watched the whiskey slosh, before, with a wrench, he tore his gaze away to consider Brodie.

'I don't know much about that night and I don't know much about anything.' He winked and tapped the side of his nose. 'But I've seen what goes on in the depot at night. I know who killed him.'

'Who?'

Worry clouded Wilfred's eyes, so Brodie moved the bottle closer, making the point that only answers would get him liquor. Wilfred leaned forward, leering and breathing stale whiskey fumes over him.

'It was the faceless man,' he declared, 'the silent spectre.'

Brodie closed his eyes for a moment.

'The faceless, silent spectre?' he intoned.

'They killed him and sent him to hell,' Wilfred babbled, his eyes darting about with manic glee. 'But I've seen him lurking in the shadows. He's returned. He killed Archibald, but if I mention his name in court, I'll die.'

'What is his name?' Brodie said, now wishing he'd not wasted his time coming here to listen to Wilfred rave.

'You didn't listen to me. Speaking his name is death.' Wilfred looked around to check nobody else was close and then leaned towards him, his voice a hoarse whisper. 'He's the devil's marshal.'

'You were right,' Brodie said as he averted his face from the acrid fumes. 'Saying that in court won't help Lucinda none.'

Wilfred chuckled and then lunged for the bottle. Brodie let him take it.

He stood up while wondering if he should complete his previous intention of trying to clean and sober up Wilfred. The determined way that Wilfred attacked the rest of the bottle convinced him that the effort would be futile.

Shaking his head, he turned away and picked his way around the discarded trash. He walked to his horse, wondering how, in the short time he had left, he could find other avenues to help his sister.

A crack sounded closely followed by two more rapid cracks, the sounds sharp and unexpected, making Brodie stop. It took him only a moment to identify the noises as having been nearby gunshots and a small, rising cloud of dust ten yards away told him they had been fired wildly towards the house.

With the high scrub providing plenty of cover around the house, Brodie lowered his head as he drew his six-shooter. His old instincts told him where the shots had been fired from, and so, without thinking, he hurried into the scrub.

Running crouched over, he reached a spot twenty yards away from the location of the shooting. He stopped to listen.

Frantic scrambling sounded, giving the impression that several men were moving quickly near by. Brodie stood tall and glimpsed the forms of three men moving behind the scrub.

He loosed off a high warning shot before lowering his gun to aim at the point where he next expected to see the men. His gunshot appeared to instil caution in the shooters as they didn't reappear and, when he heard them moving again, the sounds were some distance away and receding.

After listening for a minute to the gunmen beating a hasty retreat, he concluded that they were heading towards the depot. With the immediate danger resolved, he decided he hadn't been the shooters' target and so he hurried back to the house.

When he emerged on to clear ground, he couldn't see Wilfred and he reached the porch before he saw him lying on his back amidst the debris.

He clung on to the hope that Wilfred had just passed out until he stepped up on to the porch and saw the blood that had pooled around Wilfred's back.

In short order, he dragged Wilfred into his house, where he rested his head on a blanket. Wilfred's breathing was ragged and when Brodie raised his chin, he looked at him through eyes that were dimming rapidly.

'I told you,' Wilfred breathed, 'that speaking his name was death.'

* * *

'You have to postpone the trial now,' Brodie said.

'We don't,' Marshal Duffield said. 'Wilfred's death doesn't affect it.'

'But he was the only one man who was prepared to speak up for Lucinda, and to stop him talking he's been killed an hour before the start of the trial.'

'You don't know he was killed for that reason. Wilfred was a no-account varmint with plenty of enemies.' The marshal offered a grim smile. 'And you spoke with him. You must have gathered that what he'd say wouldn't help your sister.'

Brodie returned the smile and then headed to the law office window.

Wilfred's body was now at the undertaker's while Kyle had used up the final moments before the trial started searching for the gunmen. In the limited time, he hadn't found them and he'd left his deputy to search on his own.

'So what chance has Lucinda got for justice?'

'The same as we'd all have in her situation. She'll appear in open court and the jury will consider the evidence against her.'

Reluctantly, Brodie accepted he was powerless to help, and so he left the law office and joined the queue to enter the courtroom. An hour later, he started believing that the marshal had been right.

The case against Lucinda was even flimsier than he'd thought. Three men, who, according to the prosecution were all fine, upstanding townsfolk — a claim that filled the courtroom with applause — had spoken with Archibald Harper that night, but Archibald had been in a hurry to meet Lucinda.

Apparently, Bartholomew Stanhope, the first witness, claimed Archibald had talked to her outside the Shelby Hotel. Bartholomew didn't know why they'd arranged an assignation, although his leering look raised a knowing chuckle from the courtroom. The levity died out when he described how an argument had erupted that had degenerated into a squabble.

The men had been alarmed and they'd sent her on her way, but when Archibald had headed towards the old depot, Lucinda had chased after him into the darkness while shouting threats and promising retribution. Archibald was never seen alive again.

The cross-examination then started. Lucinda's lawyer asked Bartholomew to confirm he hadn't seen Lucinda kill Archibald. Bartholomew said he hadn't and, even though Brodie could think of a dozen ways the story could be challenged further, the lawyer then sat down.

The next two witnesses, Malachi

Moore and Levander Bass, repeated the same story in a way that, to Brodie's ears, was so similar it was if they were reading an agreed statement. Lucinda's lawyer didn't draw attention to this and instead continued the same, presumably sensible, policy of only asking each man to confirm he hadn't seen Lucinda kill Archibald.

With those statements complete, the marshal and then the doctor described how several days later, Archibald's body had been found lying in the depot.

Neither man was sure how he'd been killed. The marshal said Archibald looked as if he'd been scared to death while the doctor offered the opinion that he had been suffocated.

In an increasingly volatile atmosphere, the doctor declared that although he was unsure how Archibald could have been suffocated without leaving marks, this fact suggested that a woman rather than a man had killed him.

Brodie couldn't see how the doctor

had reached that conclusion, but it made the courtroom erupt with anger forcing the judge to clamour for calm. He didn't get it and so when the next witness arrived, she struggled to make herself heard.

Genevieve, who was introduced as the widow of Derrick Shelby, causing muttering to ripple through the court-room, said that Lucinda had completed her duties as diligently as always that evening before she'd left the hotel.

Although she hadn't seen Lucinda return, Genevieve appeared eager to say more, but the prosecution cut her short. So when Lucinda's lawyer stood up, Brodie expected he'd let her say what was on her mind, but he had no questions.

The next person to speak was Lucinda herself. This testimony proved to be an anti-climax.

Lucinda said she had talked with Archibald, but they hadn't argued; she hadn't threatened him and she hadn't followed him. Once the derision in the courtroom had died down, neither the prosecution nor the defence probed her story.

Then other witnesses stepped forward to testify to Archibald's decency, each proclamation gathering applause and murmured agreement from the courtroom.

Nobody spoke up for Lucinda, although several men who had spoken for Archibald took the stand to state that Lucinda was often seen drinking liquor and being overly friendly with men. These comments generated sorry looks with much shaking of heads, and outright abuse erupted when one witness stated that Genevieve Shelby was her best friend.

Shortly afterwards, the trial ended and the jury was sent out. It was just after noon; the trial had lasted just two hours.

Brodie was familiar enough with legal proceedings to know that the events as described didn't present a valid case against Lucinda. All they had done was raise questions, except nobody had answered them.

'What else did you want to say?' Brodie asked Genevieve after he'd followed her back to the Shelby Hotel.

Genevieve led him into a large and airy room that looked out on to the main road where she fetched them both coffees.

'Only that I hadn't known your sister for long, but she was already becoming a fine, upstanding member of the town.' She frowned. 'She's certainly a better person than the men who claimed she'd threatened Archibald.'

'It's good to hear that, and at least there was no proper evidence against her.'

'I heard nothing other than rumours and insinuations. So I can't see how . . . ' She trailed off and raised herself to look through the window. 'It appears that the jury has finished their deliberations.'

Brodie stood up and confirmed that people were hurrying back to the

31

courtroom, beckoning others to join them. Brodie bent to sip his coffee, but it was still too hot to drink.

'They've been out for only fifteen minutes,' he said. 'That has to be good news.'

Genevieve nodded and joined him in leaving the hotel. As it turned out, he was wrong on both counts. The jury had deliberated for ten minutes, and they had found Lucinda guilty.

She got thirty years.

3

'There has to be something we can do,' Brodie said, not for the first time that evening.

'If there is,' Genevieve said, 'I can't think of it, and I reckon that anything I do try won't be received well.'

She gestured at the large and empty room, as if that explained everything.

'This sure is an impressive hotel, but few people use it.' He offered a tentative smile. 'Is there something I should know?'

'My husband was a good man, but he was unpopular. After he died last year, I used his money to buy this place. I tried to make amends, but people have long memories and things were only slowly improving. Lucinda's conviction will have set me back again, so perhaps I should sell up and move on, after all.'

'If you do, another good person will

suffer through no fault of their own and prove there's no justice in this world.'

She sighed. 'Today, we both saw that's true.'

They sat in silence for a while with her final comment resounding in Brodie's mind and reinforcing the fact that what he'd seen today hadn't been justice.

Lucinda hadn't killed Archibald Harper and the evidence against her was no greater than it would have been against any person who had been picked out randomly.

'I believe in justice,' Brodie said, standing up, 'and the law isn't the only way to get it.'

His cryptic comment made Genevieve furrow her brow, but he didn't explain further. Instead he bade her good night before he retired to his room. Against expectations, he slept well, his resolution to prove his sister's innocence giving him a purpose.

The next morning he stayed in his room and through the window, watched the townsfolk come and go as he gathered a feeling for the town. Looking down on everyone from on high, he saw people talking in groups while nodding and smiling, giving him the impression that the trial had reduced the edginess he'd seen on his first night.

So at noon, he ventured out and visited the Sundown saloon and then the Four Aces, where he confirmed that his impression had been right.

Everyone was relieved that justice had been done and nobody thought the trial's briskness and lack of evidence was odd. Brodie reckoned that as a woman had been accused of killing a popular man, nobody had pursued a rigorous search for the truth and everyone had wanted the resolution that a conviction provided.

Archibald Harper's popularity stemmed from an incident eighteen months before in which, overnight, the valuable cargo of four cars had been stolen from a train in the old depot.

Nobody had ever been held responsible, although many people blamed
the local outlaw Brodie had been
pursuing, Phineas Moon. But as more
details had become known, Archibald,
the depot guard, had emerged as an
unlikely hero.

When he'd seen the masked raiders,
he had rounded up the rest of the
depot workers. Bartholomew, Malachi,
and Levander, the three witnesses who
had testified in court that they had
seen Lucinda and Archibald arguing,
had launched a daring counter-attack
against the raiders.

They'd failed. The next morning,
they'd been found tied up in one of the
warehouses, but the story of their
bravery had gathered a sympathetic
hearing.

Their popularity grew when the
railroad accepted the small depot was
inadequate and, with brave citizens
like Archibald and the others around,
the town needed a replacement,
except this time it would be bigger,

and better guarded.

The new, bustling depot on the other side of town had let Hamilton prosper, and that was down to four brave men, one of whom had now been killed.

'You look like a man,' someone said beside Brodie, breaking into his pondering, 'who's accepted he's a failure.'

From the corner of his eye, Brodie considered the newcomer. He was young, sporting a wide smile, and he wore a jaunty feather in his hat.

'I've never failed at anything,' Brodie said, deciding not to take offence. 'And I don't intend to start.'

'You already have. You were a bounty hunter with ten successful manhunts behind you, but you failed on the eleventh because a better man got to Phineas Moon first.'

'It wasn't my choice to give up looking for Phineas.' He considered the smiling young man. 'Although I'd guess you're the man who caught him.'

'Found him in Fairplay. I'm Chauncey Spurlock and Phineas provided my tenth bounty.' Chauncey tipped his hat. 'Soon, I'll have beaten your tally of hunts.'

'We're not in competition,' Brodie muttered.

'It's a good job we're not because you'd lose.'

Chauncey winked and Brodie took the opportunity to lighten his mood by ordering him a drink.

'I assume you haven't come to Hamilton to gloat.'

'Nope.' Chauncey sidled closer. 'I came to see what was on offer, but Marshal Duffield wasn't in the mood to talk.'

'That man's a fool.' Brodie waited until Chauncey nodded before continuing. 'You should move on to avoid the indignity of seeing me get ahead of you.'

Chauncey chuckled and the two men settled down at the bar in companionable silence.

Brodie relaxed, his conversation with Chauncey having helped him, even if that was by making him accept his limitations. He was a manhunter and uncovering the truth about an uncertain situation was tougher than gathering information about known quarries.

That conclusion made him bid Chauncey good day. He headed to the door. What he saw outside made his ill mood darken.

Across the road, the three witnesses who had testified against Lucinda were walking by. They were nodding to well-wishers and stopping to talk with commiserating passers-by.

He watched them until they reached the end of the road and, as these men were at the heart of the case against his sister, he followed them at a distance. He soon found that he wouldn't have to employ his skills, as their destination was obvious.

They were heading out of town to the old depot.

Brodie took a detour to reach the rise that stood beside the depot and clambered to the top. He emerged at a point that gave him a good view of the scene, letting him watch the threesome slip into one of the warehouses.

Several minutes passed during which he neither saw nor heard anything untoward, and so he raised himself to seek the best route down. A few moments later he dropped back down to hug the ground.

He wasn't the only person watching the warehouse.

When he raised himself again, he saw the darker shape of a man thirty yards down the slope. The man was on the edge of a sharper drop where the ground had fallen away and the surrounding scrub masked his form.

Brodie set off. He crawled slowly down the slope, keeping his body low and planning each movement before he made it. He aimed to emerge ten yards away from the man on the edge of the steeper ground.

After crawling for fifteen minutes, the ground became too loose for him to move silently and so he stopped to plan how he'd continue while avoiding dislodging the fragile edge, but he then discovered a more worrying problem: he could no longer see the man.

He raised himself to his knees and then to a crouching position without his target becoming visible. He had been silent and he'd heard nothing, which meant that the man had been as secretive in his movements as he had been.

He had started looking further afield when a shadow flitted nearby. Then, from the corner of his eye, he saw a darker form rise up from the scrub, but by then he was too late to stop the man turning the tables on him.

A heavy forearm slapped against the back of his neck, pushing him forward while his legs were kicked out from under him. He landed on his chest with his face driving down into the soft earth and, before he could raise his arms to push himself back up, the man settled a knee on his back, pinning him down.

Brodie turned his head, catching a

glimpse of the man's face, except he saw only shiny skin and no features before his assailant slapped a hand down on the back of his head and made him look back down. Figuring the man was determined to keep his anonymity, Brodie stilled and waited for him to make the next move, but long moments passed in which his assailant merely held him.

'Why are you watching these men?' Brodie asked. He didn't get an answer and so he persisted. 'Who are you? What do you want from me?'

None of these questions gathered a response and so he tried an alternate approach of offering information.

'No matter what anyone in town says, I reckon these men are up to no good.' This made the man shift his weight, making Brodie think he was on the right lines. 'I'm Lucinda Latimer's brother and I reckon she's innocent. I'm not leaving town until I find out who did kill Archibald.'

He waited for a response, but the

man remained silent.

'I don't have no faith in Marshal Duffield,' Brodie said as he struggled to provoke a reaction. 'I've been staying at the Shelby Hotel and — '

The man flinched and then leaned forward, but that was only so he could draw his gun. Cold metal jabbed into the back of Brodie's neck.

Figuring he had only moments to act before the man fired, he flexed his back and then bucked his assailant.

The weight lifted from his back as the man rolled aside, but Brodie's effort backfired when he pressed his hands back down on the loose earth and the ground gave way. He flailed his arms as he sought purchase, but that only made the ground slide away even faster.

Then he had a bigger problem to contend with. The ground beneath his chest dropped and he suffered a brief, dizzying sensation as he tipped over.

He fell, tumbling head over heels amidst a cascading mass of earth that had the solidity of water. As he dropped he glimpsed the slope, the warehouses, the sky, but mainly he saw dirt until the ground stilled, leaving him lying sprawled and battered.

He blinked and shook his head as he removed the grit from his eyes. When he could see again, the warehouses were towering above him, confirming he'd fallen to the bottom of the slope.

Gunfire cracked, making Brodie scramble away. He rolled over twice before settling down facing up the slope.

He couldn't see where his assailant had gone to ground, but when another shot sounded he saw dirt kick ahead of him and he realized that the shooter wasn't above him. He turned while getting to his feet to be faced with the sight of Levander Bass training a gun on him through a gap in the wall of the nearest warehouse.

Bartholomew Stanhope was kneeling in the doorway with his gun drawn while Malachi Moore had come out-side. He had braced his arm against the corner of the warehouse to take aim at him.

As Malachi fired, Brodie broke into a run. He pounded along the base of the slope, while the men in the warehouse joined Malachi in splattering gunfire along the rise above his head.

Whether they were aiming poorly or trying only to chase him off, Brodie couldn't tell, but he still concentrated on reaching the safety of the nearest cover, which turned out to be a dismantled and disintegrating fence.

He dived down behind the limited cover that the pile of rotting wood afforded and then took stock of his situation. His mystery assailant wasn't visible on the rise and with the men in the warehouse directing all their ire at him, he figured they hadn't seen him, either.

'What are you men doing out here?' Brodie shouted.

His question only encouraged the three men to spray more lead at him. Slugs hammered into the mouldering wood, which had the consistency of tightly packed paper.

Brodie figured that sustained gunfire would soon break through the fence. So instead of irritating them with more questions, he found a spot where he could watch the warehouse through a gap between two planks and then crouched down, waiting for a chance to act.

The delay gave Brodie time to think and he couldn't help but note that the three witnesses' first response was to shoot at him, suggesting they were the same men who had shot Wilfred Clay.

Five minutes passed before Malachi joined Bartholomew in the doorway, making Levander duck away to see what had concerned him. Brodie used the distraction to leap out from behind his cover and, with his head down, he sprinted towards the side wall of the warehouse.

He'd covered half the distance when Bartholomew reacted to his approach by muttering to Malachi, making him turn round. The moment they both faced him, they trained their guns on him and so, on the run, Brodie fired.

His gunshot sliced into the side of the doorway, making both men duck away. When his second shot kicked dirt between the two men, they leapt through the doorway to safety.

That was fine with Brodie as it let him reach the warehouse without further problems. He stood with his back to the wall catching his breath and then edged to the corner.

He glanced around the corner and was pleased to see his counter-attack had spooked the three men. They were hurrying away along the base of the slope with their heads down, their actions again putting Brodie in mind of the behaviour of the men who had killed Wilfred.

Angry now, he turned the tables on them by sending them on their way with rapid gunshots that sliced into the ground behind their fleeing forms, forcing them to scurry along with long, panicked strides.

The moment they'd disappeared from view, he hurried to the rise. The ground was loose and hard to climb and it took him five minutes to reach the summit, by which time the men were closing in on the outskirts of town.

The mystery assailant was no longer here.

Brodie clambered back down the rise and, at a leisurely pace, headed back to town. Even though he'd failed to find out why this meeting had taken place, when he reached town he figured he had learnt several interesting things.

The men had been quick to react violently, so they were obviously aware that someone, possibly the silent man, could be watching them. Even though that man's actions and his silence meant Brodie had gleaned no clues as to his identity, that in itself might be important.

Before he'd died, Wilfred Clay had

babbled about Archibald's killer being a man he'd called the devil's marshal. He had also referred to this man as being a faceless, silent spectre.

4

With the setting sun at his back, Brodie trooped across the road to the Shelby Hotel.

He planned to eat and drink before following up on the incident at the depot, but he stopped in the doorway when the first person he'd seen there, other than himself and Genevieve, came out.

Marshal Kyle Duffield stopped and considered Brodie with his hands on his hips and his eyes narrowed.

'I've never locked a brother and sister up at the same time,' he said, 'but carry on behaving like you are doing and you'll be in a cell, too.'

'I've done nothing wrong,' Brodie said.

'Bartholomew Stanhope says otherwise.' Kyle waited until Brodie shook his head in surprise before he continued. 'He said you tried to shoot up him and his friends and so they had to flee for their lives.'

'They fired first and then they ran, which put me in mind of the way that three gunmen had shot up Wilfred.'

Kyle shook his head, though did not appear surprised by Brodie's accusation.

'They have the right to go out to the old depot without fear of you sneaking up on them.'

Brodie folded his arms, enjoying making a revelation he assumed would surprise the marshal.

'I wasn't the only one sneaking around. Another man was watching them, silently and anonymously.'

Kyle sneered. 'You only spent a few minutes with Wilfred Clay, but clearly that was too long. He's filled your head with tales of a spectre haunting the old depot.'

Brodie was now the one who was surprised. He looked away as he collected his thoughts.

'I saw a man, not a spectre.'

'A man only you and Wilfred have seen is a spectre.'

'Even if you don't believe me, all I'm asking is that you investigate what's happening at the depot.'

'I will, and all I'm asking is that you heed this warning. Accept that your sister got justice and stop annoying good people with questions and vendettas.'

'I'll heed your warning.' Brodie waited until Kyle started to turn away. 'But I'll never accept Lucinda got justice.'

Kyle took two steps and then stopped, while looking down the road.

'She'll be picked up and escorted to Beaver Ridge Jail soon,' he said. 'I had intended to let you bid her farewell, but I've had enough of your family now. Don't give me cause to speak to you again.'

Then he moved on, leaving Brodie to head into the hotel. He presumed that the marshal had gone there to seek him out, but he found Genevieve loitering at the bottom of the stairs.

Her eyes were downcast, presumably with guilt after being caught listening to their conversation, but when she looked up, her eyes were tear-filled.

'Did the marshal upset you?' he asked.

'He tries not to,' she said, her voice small, 'I know that, but I did make him a promise.'

'What promise?'

She opened her mouth, seemingly to answer his question, but then her eyes clouded and she shook her head.

'That's none of your business.' She pointed at the dining room. 'I'll see you in there later for dinner when I'd welcome knowing how much longer you intend to stay.'

'I don't know. I plan to help Lucinda and I don't know how long that'll take. Do you need a more definite answer than that?'

She bit her bottom lip, her gaze troubled, and then turned away with his question unanswered.

Later, when Brodie ate, he again asked what was worrying her and what the marshal had said to her, but this time she rebuffed him with greater composure.

That evening he heeded the marshal's demand and he didn't question anybody in the saloons or seek out the witnesses. Instead, he headed to the depot.

Using starlight and the ambient light from the outskirts of town, he explored the main warehouse. He found nothing that explained what the meeting there had been about.

He stood by the door considering the other three warehouses, but they were further away from town and he doubted he'd be able to see well inside them. Then he flinched.

Standing between the two furthest warehouses was a man. Only his outline was visible, a hunched and still form facing him.

With his hand close to his holster, Brodie walked towards the man, expecting him to flee, but he closed in on him without a reaction. He was fifty paces away and the strain of watching a black shape in the dark made Brodie blink rapidly as he struggled to stay focused on him.

He had to walk through the shadows between the warehouses to meet him, so he expected that once he, too, was in darkness, he'd find it easier to watch him, but when he stepped out of the light from the town, he could no longer see him.

One moment he was watching the man's form, and the next he'd gone. Brodie hurried to the spot where he thought the man had been standing and here the darkness closed in.

He could hear only the light wind rustling through the depot, the distant sounds of revelry in the town, and his hammering heart. Feeling vulnerable, he swirled round. He could see nothing in all directions, but he couldn't shake off the feeling that he was being watched.

He shivered and turned away, meaning to walk calmly back into open space, but without realizing it he broke into a run and, having given into his fear, he kept running. He ran past the warehouse and then pounded out of the depot and he didn't slow until he reached the Four Aces.

He resolved to head inside and get a whiskey or three inside him, but he stopped at the door when a new sight drove away his fear.

Horses paraded down the road dragging a small metal cage set on the back of a studded and sturdy wagon. With creaking wheels and the clang of metal on metal, the wagon drew up outside the law office, the noise drawing customers out of the saloon to join Brodie.

One man drove the wagon and three riders flanked it while inside the cage sat a hunched over and chained man. Two guards dismounted and went inside. A minute later they emerged with Lucinda held between them.

She went docilely, not that there was anything she could do to fight back as she was shoved on to the back of the wagon and then into the cage. Brodie had been under the impression she would be escorted to jail separately, but she was positioned beside the current prisoner.

The moment the door was locked the wagon moved off and then trundled out of town. Brodie judged that the whole operation had taken five minutes.

'The prisoner they brought in was Phineas Moon,' Chauncey Spurlock said happily at his shoulder, 'and now he's off to Beaver Ridge Jail to get what he deserves.'

'The prisoner they brought out was my sister,' Brodie said, 'and now she's off to Beaver Ridge Jail to get what she doesn't deserve.'

His revelation made Chauncey draw in his breath sharply.

'If that was my sister,' Chauncey said after a while in a suitably neutral tone, 'I wouldn't just stand there looking annoyed.'

'I don't intend to. I'll prove she's innocent.'

'That jail has a harsh reputation. I've heard they've built a separate block for women recently, but even so . . . '

Brodie sighed. 'What else can I do other than hope she can cope until I find out who did kill Archibald Harper?'

Chauncey laid a hand on his shoulder. 'Come inside and I'll tell you what I'd do if my sister was in that cage.'

★　★　★

'Hello to the camp,' Brodie called peering ahead at the camp-fire.

'A gun's aimed at your chest and another at your head,' a harsh voice said from the darkness somewhere to his right. 'State your business and then leave.'

Brodie raised his hands. 'I'm not trouble. I just want to share your fire.'

'Nobody who doesn't like trouble would want to spend the night with us.'

Brodie coughed, trying to garner sympathy. Fortunately, the cough grated the back of his throat and, unable to control his breathing, he barked out several more coughs, forcing him to bend over and lower his hands to his knees while he took long, soothing breaths.

He sensed men moving closer in the darkness as his actions clearly generated only suspicion and so, while he still had a chance, he took a step closer to the fire and spoke quickly.

'If I move on, I'll freeze to death before I can light a fire. I don't care what you men are doing. I just want to get warm.'

A man stepped into the light and looked him up and down. Brodie hunched down making his form as small and unthreatening as he could.

Brusquely, the man frisked him. Then he went to his horse to check for weapons. He found his Peacemaker, which made him pause before he came back, nodding.

'Get warm,' he declared. 'Do anything else and you'll join our friends in the cage.'

'Beaver Ridge Jail,' a man said from the darkness, 'don't care about paperwork, so don't expect them to notice if there's one more man in there.'

This comment made several men laugh. Brodie provided a worried expression, as if he'd been unaware these men were escorting prisoners. Then he busied himself with doing what he'd claimed he'd wanted to do by staying on the periphery of the camp and getting warm.

When nobody was looking his way, he studied his temporary colleagues. Two men sat around the fire in pensive silence. He couldn't see the other two men, although after an hour guard duties swapped and they left to stand lookout.

He couldn't see the prisoners in the cage, as it had been set away from the fire where they couldn't enjoy the heat. They had been granted one small act of kindness; a canvas sheet had been thrown over the bars to protect them from the chill wind.

When he'd learnt everything he could about the guards' procedures, Brodie went to his horse. He did so openly with his hands raised and slowly removed an almost empty whiskey bottle. When he returned to the fire, he nursed the dregs as he trod the fine line between hiding what he was drinking and ensuring he drew attention to it.

It took ten minutes before a guard he'd heard being called Patrick came over and considered him with less distrust than the others had.

'You need something like that in you on a night like this,' Patrick said while batting his hands against his arms in a show of trying to warm up.

Brodie drew the bottle up to the light to show he had only a few mouthfuls left. Then, with a shrug, he held it out.

Patrick took the bottle and, with a gleam in his eye, upended it. As the whiskey disappeared down his throat,

Brodie leapt to his feet, but when Patrick raised a warning hand he backed away.

After emptying the bottle, Patrick smacked his lips and then hurled the bottle into the night. As glass tinkled, he faced Brodie with his hands on his hips, daring him to complain.

'In that case,' Brodie grumbled, 'I'll sit closer to the fire.'

He moved to go by Patrick, but a hand clamped down on his shoulder.

'You got any more rotgut?'

'No. You drank up my supply.'

Brodie shuffled on for a few paces before picking a spot where he could sit as far away from the guards as possible while still staying within the circle of firelight. The other guard, Silas, had been watching the exchange with lively interest and so when Patrick returned to his position, Silas raised the point Brodie had expected.

'He's a liar,' Silas said. 'I looked in his bags and he had two more bottles.'

Patrick turned on his heel quickly. He

returned, clinking the two full bottles together, although he stopped beside Brodie and, with mock generosity, held one out.

'You want to drink our whiskey?' he asked.

'Obliged,' Brodie muttered, taking the bottle.

His sullen attitude made the guards laugh before they sat together and passed the other bottle back and forth.

Brodie put the bottle to his lips and, as nobody was paying him close attention, let the brew dribble down his chin before he wiped his face with his sleeve. Then he bent over the bottle in a protective way and turned away from the fire.

He gave the impression he was drinking slowly, while in reality he dripped the liquid on to the ground. When the guard duty changed, the new men wasted no time in seizing his bottle, and so Brodie found a comfortable and warm place to lie.

With his eyes closed he lay on his

63

back and listened to the contented chatter that rose in volume as the liquor level dropped. Later, the men changed duties again, a process that this time produced plenty of good-natured, inebriated banter.

They didn't change guard duty again.

Brodie still waited until he heard enough snoring to know that the liberal quantity of sleeping draught he'd decanted into the whiskey had taken its toll. Then he got to his feet and pattered around the guards until he found the key to the cage.

He then faced the problem of how he could free his sister while not freeing the other prisoner. So he collected his Peacemaker before moving over to the wagon.

He ducked down and looked beneath the canvas, but he could see only a thin sliver of the two prisoners' forms, lying still as they slept. He slipped on to the back of the wagon and then raised the bottom of the canvas.

This increased the loudness of the

snoring, but the bulk of the cage was still in shadow. He leaned closer, letting him discern the forms lying sprawled in the cage. Both prisoners appeared to be constrained by chains attached to the base.

As he couldn't see enough to work out which figure was Lucinda, he raised the canvas higher and approached the bars. In a sudden blur of motion, Phineas Moon's grinning face rose up before him as he kicked the cage door open to slam it into Brodie's chest, knocking him aside.

While Brodie was still reeling in surprise that the door had been unlocked, Phineas stuck a hand through the bars and clamped it around his neck. Then he dragged Brodie up to the bars.

Brodie struggled and, with one hand gripping a bar and the other wrapped around the wrist at his throat, he tore his neck free. Before he could move away, Phineas stepped through the open door clutching a bunched coil of chains, which he slapped against the side of Brodie's head with a dull thud.

Feeling numb and unable to control his motion, Brodie dropped to the base of the wagon where he lay groaning.

Hands pattered over his clothes. A cry of triumph sounded in the dark as his gun was claimed, but the sound appeared to be coming from some distance away.

Then a deeper darkness stole over him.

5

'You have to move,' Lucinda insisted, tugging his arm. 'They'll be coming for us.'

'Go away,' Brodie murmured. He tore his arm free, but his first response after regaining consciousness encouraged her. She grabbed both his arms and dragged him along the ground.

Brodie ploughed through the dirt on his back until, with an exasperated grunt, Lucinda released him and fell to the ground. They lay beside each other breathing deeply until Brodie's befuddled senses came into focus. He sat up and looked down at Lucinda, who mustered a smile.

'I was worried you'd never come to,' Lucinda said.

'Where are we?' Brodie looked around, seeing only the spooky outline of the nearby starlit scrub waving in the wind. 'What happened?'

'Phineas knocked you out. He stole a horse and ran the rest off to delay the guards. I hid until he'd gone. Then I helped you.' Lucinda stood up and peered into the darkness. 'But I wasn't strong enough to move you far and the guards won't be sleeping for long.'

'You're right.' Brodie rubbed his head. 'But tell me one thing: was Phineas about to escape?'

Lucinda sighed. 'Phineas had a key and he planned to sneak away when the time was right. You gave him an opportunity. Is that enough chatter for now?'

Brodie nodded and then held out a hand for Lucinda to help him to his feet. Then they set off with his sister leading.

Lucinda had a direction in mind and so Brodie didn't waste his energies questioning her. While he shook off the effects of having been knocked out, he concentrated on putting one foot in front of the other.

After running for fifteen minutes, he stopped feeling disorientated although an insistent hammering still pounded in his head. To take his mind off his discomfort, he told Lucinda about his experiences since he'd last seen her, concentrating on Wilfred's demise and his subsequent encounter with the witnesses.

'Do you have any idea,' he asked, finishing off his story, 'who the silent man could be?'

Lucinda ran on for a while before she called a halt. They had reached high ground where they could look down on the winding river that ultimately passed to the north of Hamilton. The water glittered in the starlight, although the low, thundering rumble that drifted up to them showed that the river wasn't as inviting as it looked.

'I don't know. I hadn't been in town for long and Archibald was the first man I'd got to know well.'

With her offering no more suggestions, Brodie looked at the water.

'Downriver or upriver?' he asked, accepting that the water provided an insurmountable barrier.

'Neither,' Lucinda said with relish. 'We go across. When the guards round up their horses, they'll never get them across a river that wide and that lively.'

'That's a good plan.' Brodie waited until Lucinda's teeth gleamed in the starlight before he continued. 'Except for one problem: I can't swim.'

'Swimming is just floating at speed,' she said with a shrug. 'I'll help you across.'

Lucinda moved on down the slope and so, encouraged by his sister's optimism, Brodie followed, but the closer they got to the river, the greater became his misgivings. The roar of the water grew in volume and the churning on the surface became more obvious, promising him that this was the worst place to embark on his first attempt at swimming.

Desperate to find an alternative, he stopped and looked around. Upriver, the ground rose, presenting an expanse of dark rock while the lower ground downriver was featureless other than for the undulating scrub. So he looked back along the route they'd taken and that made him wince.

Riders stood at the top of the rise in the place where he and Lucinda had stopped ten minutes ago. Clearly the guards had rounded up their horses quickly. Brodie looked back down the slope.

Lucinda had gone to ground and so he crouched down, too, but it was already too late to remain undetected, as the riders moved off down the slope towards him.

Brodie swung round and hurried away, his scrambling progress making enough noise for Lucinda to peer out from behind a mound fifty yards on. Brodie ran on, but he couldn't help but look back at the riders, who had already covered a quarter of the distance to him.

He judged that they wouldn't close

the gap before they reached the water, but Lucinda gestured at him to join her behind the mound.

'What's wrong?' Brodie asked when he'd pounded to a halt.

Lucinda pointed down and so Brodie edged forward. He winced when he confirmed that what he'd taken to be a steady incline was in fact an abrupt drop of fifty feet down to the water.

Lucinda skirted along between the mound and the edge and he followed. Unfortunately, that gave him an uninterrupted view of the river edge and for several hundred yards there was just a sheer drop.

'It's not that far down,' Lucinda said, her nervous tone belying her words, 'and the water will be deep below us.'

Brodie slapped a firm hand on his sister's shoulder and gripped it.

'You might make it, but I won't.'

'We have no other option. We have to . . . ' Lucinda trailed off as she clearly registered Brodie's sombre tone that acknowledged what their other option was. 'I'm not leaving you.'

'It's your only hope.' Brodie pointed up the slope where hoof beats were thudding closer. 'I don't reckon the guards saw you and I won't tell them where you went.'

'I effectively got life imprisonment, but you freed two prisoners. You're facing a sentence, too.' Lucinda held out a hand. 'We jump together.'

Brodie considered her hand as he heard the horses draw to a halt on the other side of the mound. He nodded, making Lucinda bend forward over the edge as she searched for the best place to leap.

Brodie joined her and confirmed that the water was surging by below. Then he shoved Lucinda firmly in the back, toppling her over the edge.

He craned his neck to watch her plummet down into the water and he held his breath until he saw her bob back up. Then the strong current dragged her away, but he caught glimpses of her flailing arms and so was confident she was swimming effectively.

He moved along the edge as he considered how he could remain free for as long as possible to give Lucinda the best chance. He didn't get far.

The mound ended a dozen yards on and he'd yet to reach it when Silas stepped out before him with a gun already drawn. Brodie's only consolation was that he looked only at him and not downwards.

So with Lucinda now swimming off downriver, he turned round hoping to keep Silas's attention on him as he was escorted back to clear ground, but just then, Patrick appeared at the other end of the mound.

'Jump if you want to,' Patrick said, 'but you'll be full of lead before you hit the water.'

'In that case,' Brodie said, as he raised his hands and moved on, 'I'll surrender.'

'Where are the prisoners?' Patrick asked when Brodie had stepped out beyond the mound.

Brodie bit his bottom lip to avoid sighing with relief as he got confirmation that Lucinda hadn't been noticed.

'I haven't seen anyone since the breakout,' he said.

⋆   ⋆   ⋆

Daylight found Brodie locked in the cage.

His guards had been irritated to find they'd followed a trail that had led only to him and so they'd returned to the campsite. In the light, they'd picked up Phineas's trail and so the pursuit had got underway.

As the wagon trundled along, he comforted himself with the thought that his captors hadn't been aware of how close they'd been to capturing his sister, although that relief was tinged with fear, as he was unsure about her fate.

As the day wore on, the pursuit turned out to be a winding one as Phineas either backtracked or covered his path, until, late in the day, the guards stopped to discuss tactics. The result of this meeting was that Patrick and Silas stayed with him while the other two headed off at speed, unencumbered by the cage.

That night when he was fed Brodie tried to talk with his captors, but he was ignored. So with nothing to occupy his mind, he resorted to observing their actions while hoping a chance to escape would present itself.

It didn't, as after his previous successful subterfuge, Patrick and Silas took no chances during their sullen and slow pursuit of the other guards. Before long, Brodie stopped looking for opportunities.

His internment became a seemingly endless time spent jostling about in the cage during the day or spent huddling up at night trying to get warm. He'd lost track of the passage of time and so he couldn't decide if it was the fifth day since his capture or the sixth when he started to recognize landmarks.

It was dark when the wagon clattered into Hamilton and drew up outside the law office. Silas fetched the deputy, who escorted Brodie inside and deposited him on a chair before the marshal's desk.

Fifteen minutes passed before Marshal Kyle Duffield arrived. The marshal removed his handcuffs and then considered him until the guard left.

'I never expected you'd act so stupidly,' Kyle said when the wagon had rattled away. 'A murderous woman is at large and the outlaw Phineas Moon is free again to raise hell. Any crimes they commit before they're caught will be your fault.'

'As long as my sister's free,' Brodie said, his head lowered and with a croaking voice after having spoken only rarely recently, 'I don't care about my punishment.'

He heard a rustling and then a clink before Kyle sat back, but when he looked up, he wasn't sure what the marshal had done. Then he saw where

Kyle was looking.

He'd removed his star and placed it in the centre of his desk.

'You sure will suffer,' Kyle said before winking. 'You're Hamilton's new marshal.'

Brodie stared at Kyle agog until he decided his journey's prolonged tedium had numbed his senses.

'My sense of humour has taken a knock recently,' he said. 'You'll have to explain that joke.'

'No joke.' With an outstretched finger Kyle moved the star closer to Brodie. 'Three weeks ago I told the mayor that after Archibald Harper's murderer had been convicted, I'd resign as town marshal and move on. He accepted my decision, but with one stipulation: that I pick my successor. I pick you.'

'Why me?' Brodie spluttered.

'Because nobody wants the job.' Kyle smiled and kept his lips unturned until Brodie returned the smile.

'I can see you're desperate, but I'm no lawman.'

'You have a yearning to uncover the truth.'

'I was motivated, but I still learnt nothing. I proved that I'm a man-hunter, not someone who works out who's guilty in the first place.'

'Then your experiences will have prepared you for the disappointments that'll dog your every day.' Kyle raised a hand when Brodie started to object again. 'But you've misunderstood. I'm not asking you. I'm telling you that if you don't accept, I'll charge you with every crime I can think of for freeing Phineas and your sister.'

Brodie closed his eyes for a few moments to compose himself and then sat up straight.

'And all I have to do to avoid jail is be your successor?'

'That and complete your first duty as a lawman.' Kyle licked his lips. 'Bring your sister to justice.'

Brodie had been starting to nod, accepting that this surprising appoint-ment gave him a chance to uncover the truth about Archibald's murder and perhaps even capture Phineas, but the last comment made him wince.

'I can't do that. Lucinda's innocent.'

Kyle pushed the star forward again so that it sat on the edge of the desk; his intense gaze promised that he relished making his next comment.

'This morning, Bartholomew Stanhope turned up dead. This evening, nobody can find Malachi Moore. So the remaining witness, Levander Bass, fears for his life, as does the jury and — '

'I can't say I'm concerned to hear that, but Lucinda wouldn't use her freedom to take revenge on the men who testified against her.'

Kyle spread his hands. 'So find out who is killing them, or find Lucinda. Either way, Hamilton needs its marshal.'

With his gaze set on Kyle, Brodie reached out, but he stopped with his fingers spread out over the star.

'Does the outgoing marshal have any

advice for the new marshal?'

Kyle smiled now that he knew he had him.

'Justice is blind. It cares not for friendship, for loyalty, for . . . for love.'

Brodie nodded and then scooped up the star.

'In other words,' he said as he pinned the badge on his chest, 'act like the devil's own marshal?'

He waited until Kyle balked at his comment and then headed out of his law office.

6

'Who is the devil's marshal?' Brodie asked when Genevieve Shelby brought him the coffee he'd ordered.

The question made Genevieve go as pale as Kyle had gone and, when she joined him in the large, empty dining room, she knocked into the table, almost toppling his mug.

'I haven't heard anyone use that insult for a long time,' she said. 'Where did you hear it?'

'Wilfred Clay mentioned him.'

She sighed and took calming breaths.

'Wilfred often struggled to avoid his wrath.' Genevieve frowned. 'But the version you'll hear from me will be different to the one that others will tell you. People called my husband the devil's marshal. He was our lawman before Kyle Duffield.'

Brodie winced and, while he struggled

to provide a suitable response, he looked around the huge room, again feeling surprised he was the only guest there.

'I'm surprised others don't remember him kindly,' he said finally. 'Aside from the recent deaths, Hamilton is clearly a peaceful town and I'm sure that's not Kyle's work.'

She smiled, relaxing for the first time since he'd mentioned her husband.

'Derrick was a strong, determined man. He needed to be. The first marshal they appointed, Gideon Gale, didn't see out his first day and so they brought in someone who could tame this town. But the swift justice he handed out at the end of a Peacemaker made more enemies than friends.'

She lowered her head, seemingly unwilling to explain more.

'How did he die?' Brodie asked, reckoning that even if she were reluctant to provide details, she'd answer this question.

'His deputy back then, Kyle, found

him lying in the depot. He'd been shot in the head.'

'What was he investigating?'

She raised her head to consider him and then nodded with approval at his line of questioning.

'The depot raid six months earlier. He wasn't convinced the story everyone else believed was the truth. He reckoned Archibald and the others had masterminded the raid, not tried to prevent one. That belief caused his popularity to plummet as those men's lot rose.' She smiled when Brodie raised an intrigued eyebrow. 'But nobody was found responsible and, in truth, it could have been any number of people.'

'And he's buried in the cemetery outside town?'

'Of course he . . . ' She narrowed her eyes. 'I hope you didn't believe Wilfred's tales about my husband's ghost haunting the old depot.'

'I didn't, but I do believe Wilfred saw someone lurking around, because I saw him, too.'

She waggled a finger at him. 'Whoever you saw, it wasn't Derrick. My husband died. Half of the town attended his funeral, even if many came to be sure he was dead.'

Brodie took a deep breath, unwilling to ask her to clarify, but he figured his new job would require him to ask uncomfortable questions. So he placed a hand over hers.

'Did you see his body?'

'No.' She met his gaze with a determination that showed she wanted to refute the conclusion she knew he'd draw. 'Kyle identified him and he said the sight wouldn't do me no good, so the coffin remained closed.'

'So you only had Kyle's word about the way he died,' Brodie mused. 'And now Archibald has died, too, in mysterious circumstances at the depot.'

She slipped her hand away. 'If you're thinking that whoever killed my husband killed Archibald, too, it's possible. But if you're thinking that my husband feigned his own death and he killed

Archibald, you should hand that star in now.'

'I don't intend to hand in my star just yet.'

She accepted his answer with a nod. 'Then you're welcome to use your room for as long as I'm still here.'

'You're thinking of moving on?'

Genevieve gestured at her clothing. 'I'm still a young woman and I hate wearing black. I promised myself and others that a year would be long enough to mourn. That year ended last Friday and as there's nothing for me here, perhaps now is the right time to start a new life . . .'

She trailed off, her eyes watering.

'I'll be sorry to see you leave. Can I do anything to encourage more people to stay here and improve your situation?'

'The people who didn't like my husband have long memories and loud voices. The rest have short memories and weak minds.' She looked around the empty room, her less troubled gaze clearly recalling good memories. 'Before the previous owner died, the hotel held dances and for a while that made this room the centre of town.'

'I remember going to dances with Lucinda when I was younger. They were the best nights of the week and they brought the whole town together.' He shrugged. 'Perhaps you should hold a dance in here again, as one last attempt to change everything.'

She shook her head. 'Nobody would come.'

'Then this room will be as empty as it was before. You'll have lost nothing and when you leave, you'll have the comfort of knowing you did everything you could to make the hotel prosper.'

She opened her mouth to reply, but her voice croaked with emotion and so she mustered a wan smile before pointing at the door. She got to her feet and walked away with calm dignity until whatever emotion he'd stirred up with his suggestion got the better of her and she hurried from the room, sobbing.

When he'd heard her head into her quarters, Brodie supped the remainder of his coffee and then left the hotel. It was late in the evening, but as a light was burning in the surgery, he went in to speak with Doctor Taylor.

The doctor had no patients other than the dead Bartholomew Stanhope. Taylor removed the sheet to reveal Bartholomew staring upwards with unseeing eyes and with a mouth that was open so wide, it was as if his jaw had been broken.

'Is this how Archibald looked?' Brodie asked.

'Yes,' Taylor said. He rocked his head from side as he went round to the other side of the body. 'As Kyle said, it looks as if he was scared to death.'

'I'd expect more from a medical man,' Brodie snapped. He set his hands on his hips. 'How exactly did Archibald die and was Bartholomew killed in the same way?'

'I reckon they were both suffocated,

although I can't work out how.' Taylor pointed down into Bartholomew's mouth. 'And they both had their tongues cut out.'

Brodie winced as he peered into the empty maw of Bartholomew's mouth.

'The silent man,' he mused.

'He would have been. I reckon it was removed while he was still alive.'

'To stop him talking?' Brodie said. 'Or as punishment for talking?'

'You'll have to figure that one out for yourself. I just report on how they died.'

'So are there any other similarities between the two deaths?'

Doc Taylor replaced the sheet and then considered.

'They both went missing for a while before they were found. They were both dirty, as if they'd been held somewhere unpleasant, they'd both been suffocated and had their tongues removed, and they both had a shocked expression, as if they'd died of fright.'

'And they both used to work at the

old depot and both became popular after they tried to foil the train raid.'

'Yes,' Taylor said in a deliberate manner as if he accepted this was important. 'Which reminds me that Kyle Duffield found both bodies at the depot. I guess if Malachi Moore is lying dead out there waiting to be discovered, too, it'll soon become clearer whether those similarities are important or coincidences.'

Brodie nodded and, after telling Doc Taylor to inform him if he uncovered any more important details, he left the surgery. Outside, he stood on the boardwalk listening to the lively sounds coming from the saloons while pondering on what he'd learnt in the hour since his appointment.

He moved off, just as splinters burst from the corner post to his side, the blast of gunfire only registering a moment later. He jerked to the side and drew his six-shooter, but when he saw movement in an alley opposite, he broke into a run.

He ran across the road to a spot beside the alley where he waited with his back to the wall. Within the alley, feet pounded a retreat and so he swung into the entrance.

Silhouetted against the lighter night sky beyond was the form of a fleeing man. He had the same build as his silent assailant who he now thought of as being the devil's marshal.

This time, he levelled his gun on the man's back and fired, but the devil's marshal appeared to detect that Brodie was there and he twisted and dropped to one knee. As Brodie's slug clattered into the alley wall, the man fired and so, in self-preservation, Brodie threw himself aside, gaining the safety of the road.

Then, before the devil's marshal could move on, he slipped his arm around the corner and fired blindly and quickly, aiming low and splaying his gunfire around the alley. He reloaded and then swung into the alley, crouched down.

From his low position, he couldn't

see the gunman and neither did he have a clear view of the whole alley, forcing him to move on cautiously in case the man had gone to ground in the shadows. It took him a minute to reach the other end during which time he heard nothing and encountered no one.

When he risked glancing beyond the corner of the alley at the backs of the buildings, all was still. He went left, heading for the old depot.

On the way he didn't see the devil's marshal and he didn't slow until he reached the corner of the nearest warehouse. The light was as poor as it had been the last time he'd gone there at night and he couldn't help but look first at the place where he thought he'd seen someone before.

This time nobody was there, but the recollection made him stop. He took deep breaths, his heart pounding and coldness creeping over him. He tried to move on, but his legs felt leaden and he was reluctant to explore further.

He shook himself, but that only made

him feel he was being watched. He turned away as a gunshot blasted and he heard wood splinter as the slug hammered into the wall above his head.

A second shot sliced into the ground at his feet while a third hit the wall, this time closing in on him. The shots had been fired so rapidly it made him feel as if he'd walked into an ambush.

No longer feeling foolish for having become spooked, he beat a hasty retreat. Several more wild gunshots hurried him on his way, but they petered out when he closed in on the town.

He went straight to the Four Aces. He ordered a whiskey and, as his heart was still pounding from his flight, he knocked it back in a gulp before ordering a second. Only then did he turn to find that all eyes in the saloon were on him.

'So this is our new marshal,' Levander Bass declared, stepping forward from amongst a group of customers. 'The gun-toting brother of a convicted killer who finds the courage to see us in a whiskey bottle.'

Numerous customers grunted their support for this view, but Brodie ignored them. He put down his glass and walked up to Levander.

'There's been several unexplained killings and Kyle Duffield couldn't cope,' he said levelly, his comment pleasingly gathering a few knowing murmurs. 'I intend to succeed where he failed.'

His comment made Levander lower his gaze and so Brodie returned to the bar to knock back his drink. He was wondering whether to order another to reinforce the point that he'd leave only when he chose to, when Levander found his voice.

'Enjoy your first evening in here as a lawman, Marshal. I don't reckon you'll survive for long enough to enjoy a second.'

Brodie turned slowly, ensuring he kept a thin smile on his lips.

'Your prediction makes me wonder if

you once said that to Derrick Shelby.'

'Don't make accusations when Bartholomew's dead, Malachi's gone missing and your sister is at large again.'

'She is, but Lucinda is no fool. She'll have high-tailed it away from here and she'll never return, but either way I wouldn't have expected to see you cowering in your boots at the prospect of my little sister coming after you.' Brodie leaned forward when his comment made several customers laugh. 'So who are you really scared of?'

Levander glanced away to look out the window and even when he turned back he picked at a stray thread on his sleeve as he presumably thought about his reply.

'I heard how Bartholomew died,' he said to fill the silence. 'It worried me.'

'It should do. He died in the same way as Archibald died, and I can't help but note that Archibald, Bartholomew, Malachi, and you were all involved in trying to foil the train raid eighteen months ago.'

Levander gulped. 'We acted for the good of this town.'

'You did. So have you seen someone recently that you haven't seen since those days?' Brodie waited, but Levander didn't reply and so, with his patience wearing thin, he prompted, 'Such as the devil's marshal?'

Levander snorted. 'Derrick Shelby died.'

'So they say, but I've heard that his spectre is haunting the depot and it's death to even utter his name, except I don't believe in ghosts and I'm starting to wonder if he didn't die after all.'

Levander didn't move a muscle, his determination to avoid reacting telling its own story. After a lengthy silence, he released his breath with a long sigh and then aimed a stern finger at Brodie.

'I don't have to talk to you about something that happened long before you got pinned to that star.'

'You do. That investigation is still

open.' Brodie turned to the door. He took a single step away and then stopped. 'Talk to me while you still have a tongue in your head.'

Levander didn't retort, but Brodie figured they'd exchanged enough views for now and he left the saloon.

He returned to the Shelby Hotel along roads that were filling with people spilling out of the saloons. He encountered no further trouble, although he didn't expect any from a man who took pot shots at unsuspecting targets before running away.

Other than the reception room, the hotel was dark confirming that Genevieve had retired for the night. He headed straight up to his room. Mindful that a dark and deserted place was an ideal location for the devil's marshal to attack him again, he walked quietly.

Before he reached his room, he heard movement coming from within. He stopped beside the door and listened, hearing someone pacing back and forth across the room.

He waited until the intruder had reached the window side of the room and then moved sideways to stand before the door. He kicked it open.

In a moment he picked out the form of the person inside and swung his gun up to shoulder height, but he didn't fire.

The intruder was his sister.

7

'Why did you come back here?' Brodie asked when he and Lucinda had both calmed down after the shock of their initial meeting.

'I had nowhere else to go,' Lucinda said with a shrug, 'and Genevieve was the only person I could think of who might hide me and then lend me money to escape.'

'And has she?'

'I haven't asked her yet.' She sat in the chair by the window and offered a smile. 'I sneaked up here and hid, but now that I've seen you, I'll face that problem tomorrow.'

Brodie returned Lucinda's smile before tapping his star and providing a stern expression.

'Whether you do that as a free woman or as my first prisoner depends on the answer to one question.'

Lucinda stared at his star, her eyebrows raised in surprise, confirming she hadn't noticed his change in status before.

'Are you really a lawman?' she said finally.

Brodie sighed with relief, judging that her comment meant she didn't know what his important question was.

'Kyle Duffield resigned and he needed a replacement. The only man he could find to take over was someone he could threaten with a jail sentence.' Brodie waited until Lucinda provided a supportive frown. 'My first tasks are to find Bartholomew Stanhope's killer and the missing Malachi Moore.'

Lucinda nodded slowly until the implication registered and she winced.

'I didn't kill Bartholomew, if that's your one question.'

'It is,' Brodie said. He spoke quickly when his confirmation made Lucinda scowl. 'But now I know for sure you didn't, we'll prove you're innocent and find the man who did do it.'

'We will, and if other people are being killed, it might explain why Archibald died.' Lucinda slapped the chair arm in frustration. 'But I can't figure that out hiding up here.'

'You can't leave. The townsfolk's mood says you won't survive for five minutes on your own. So tell me everything you know and hopefully something you say will lead me to the culprit.'

His positive outlook enthused Lucinda and she relaxed enough to talk about her life in Hamilton and then her brief, doomed relationship with Archibald Harper. She also described what she knew about the conflicts in town.

This added nothing to what he'd learnt already, but Brodie didn't prompt her. He hoped that what she offered freely would either bolster or demolish his theory that Archibald's death was connected to Marshal Derrick Shelby's apparent murder.

By the time Lucinda ran out of steam, they'd talked late into the night and so she claimed the bed while he slept sitting up in the chair by the window. She was asleep within moments and Brodie soon joined her.

In the morning, he sought out Genevieve. He found her standing outside talking with Kyle Duffield. When Kyle saw him coming, he made his excuses and left.

Afterwards, Genevieve was as preoccupied as she had been the last time she'd spoken with the former marshal, but Brodie's revelation that his sister was hiding in his room didn't concern her. She promised to allocate Lucinda a separate room and take her up a meal and a change of clothes.

With that, Brodie started his first full day as a lawman by talking to people about the missing Malachi Moore. Nobody had any useful information about where he might be, but most people treated him with respect with only a few being surly, presumably due to his sister's alleged crime.

He finished his patrol in the Four

Aces where he headed to the bar to join one man he hadn't expected to see again — the bounty hunter Chauncey Spurlock.

'Why are you still here?' Brodie said.

'Phineas Moon has escaped and I've heard he's nearby,' Chauncey said with his usual grin. He glanced at Brodie's star. 'But I didn't think you'd go to such lengths to stop me beating your bounty tally.'

Brodie sighed, this reminder of the escaped prisoner only adding to his woes.

'I didn't want this appointment, but as I'm a lawman now, I won't gain from the outlaws I arrest.'

Chauncey shrugged. 'Then prepare to be beaten soon, whether by me finding Phineas or by . . . '

Chauncey left his sentiment unfinished, but Brodie caught his meaning.

'The other escaped prisoner is my sister.' Brodie pointed a stern finger at Chauncey. 'Go after her and you'll never beat my tally.'

Chauncey limited his response to a brief nod and so, having accomplished what he'd set out to achieve with his first patrol, Brodie headed to the law office where, for the second time that morning, he met Kyle. He was sitting on a corner of his old desk and chatting with Deputy Erskine Farlow as if he'd never retired.

'How's your first day going?' Kyle asked.

'It was going well,' Brodie said. 'Have you got a reason for being here?'

Kyle clearly picked up on his sour mood, as he stood up and then moved away from his desk.

'I've come in here every day for over a year,' he said. 'It's a hard habit to break.'

'Tomorrow might be the day you try harder.'

Kyle frowned and then looked at Erskine, who provided support with a surly glare and folded arms.

'I can be useful to you,' Kyle said with a neutral tone. 'While you were in the saloon, I found Malachi Moore's body.'

'Out at the old depot and killed like Bartholomew and Archibald were, I presume?'

'Yeah. Looked like he was scared to death, but with no marks on him other than his tongue having been cut out; dirty, missing for a while — '

'And found by you.'

Kyle pointed at him. 'Don't waste your breath on insinuations when you're not doing your job. You now have three unsolved murders, two of which involve popular townsfolk. That's made Levander Bass go into hiding because he doesn't trust the new marshal to keep him safe.'

Brodie walked up to Kyle, his anger growing by the minute. When Kyle stood his ground, with a snarl he grabbed his collar and walked him across the office until he slammed his back against the wall.

Erskine moved towards them, but Kyle raised a hand, bidding him to stay back. That didn't reduce Brodie's irritation.

'You're right,' he snarled. 'I'm not making progress, but there're five outstanding murders.'

Kyle furrowed his brow until, with a scowl, he acknowledged he'd caught some of his meaning.

'Your sister may still be at large, but the court decided her guilt. What's the fifth murder?'

'Your predecessor, Derrick Shelby.' Brodie dragged Kyle forward and then slammed him back against the wall for emphasis. 'I reckon his death is connected to the train raid and that's the key to solving what's happening now.'

Kyle gulped and glanced away, perhaps showing that his theory hadn't surprised him, but it turned out to be a subterfuge when he tore himself free. He side-stepped away for a pace giving him enough room to thud a low punch into Brodie's side, but from close quarters he couldn't get much force behind the blow.

Brodie shook off the punch and then swung Kyle round. He delivered a backhanded slap to Kyle's face that sent him sprawling over his desk before he tipped over it to land on the other side.

Erskine moved in, but he stilled when Brodie shot him a warning glare. Then Brodie moved around the desk and bent down to draw Kyle up off the floor.

'Derrick's spectre,' Kyle said defiantly, shaking him off, 'hasn't returned to take revenge.'

'I know. The killer is very much alive. I've seen him.'

'Only you and Wilfred have seen this man roaming around the depot.'

'Several men who are now dead saw him, too.' He waited until Kyle conceded his point with a narrowing of the eyes and then gestured at the door. 'But if you're ever minded to offer me unwanted advice again, don't.'

'I won't. I've had my fill of Hamilton and I'm leaving on Saturday.' Kyle used the desk to draw himself to his feet and then batted the dust from his knees before he smiled triumphantly. 'If you haven't made an arrest by then, I'll leave a letter on the mayor's desk telling him you freed the prisoners. That means you have two days before you end up in a cell.'

Kyle jutted his jaw, giving Brodie the impression he wanted him to say he was under suspicion and he couldn't leave. But Brodie provided only a benign expression, giving Kyle no option other than to walk out of the office.

Brodie waited until the door was closed before he faced Deputy Farlow.

'That felt good,' he said, flexing his fists. 'Now show me Kyle's reports. I want to learn about this town.'

Erskine went over to a large cupboard and removed a folder, which he threw on to Brodie's desk.

'Kyle's records,' he said.

'Is this all of them?' Brodie asked eyeing the slim wad of papers.

'Kyle was a fine lawman. He didn't

waste his time on concerns that don't matter none.'

'I never said he should have, but I was hoping to read more details about Derrick Shelby's death.'

'Nobody cared who killed him back then and nobody remembers him now. Spend your time working out who killed the people who matter, like Bartholomew and now Malachi.'

Brodie looked at the piles of yellowing reports in the cupboard, these presumably being Derrick Shelby's records.

'I intend to do both,' he said. 'But as I like plain speaking, if something's on your mind, say it.'

Erskine provided an affirmative grunt. 'Kyle took me on after Derrick's demise. I've worked hard and well, so when he left I thought I'd be standing where you are now.'

'Obliged for your honesty. Now, find out where Levander has holed up and, before you report back, work out whether you want to carry on standing where you are now. It don't matter none to me what you decide. I'm used to working alone.'

Erskine looked aloft as he presumably searched this order for hidden traps.

'Then you intend to keep Levander safe, do you?'

'No. I intend to question him. If I don't like his answers, I'll arrest him.'

8

As Brodie read Derrick Shelby's reports, he became impressed by the former lawman's record-keeping and by the man himself. From Derrick's strong handwriting and his even stronger choice of words, Brodie gathered an impression of a no-nonsense man who was never troubled by self-doubt.

Archibald and the others had spirited away the train cargo. Then they'd tied themselves up and invented the story of masked raiders stealing the cargo despite their bravery.

Derrick had no evidence to support what to him were facts, so he chronicled their activities as he waited for them to make a mistake.

His only source of rumours was Wilfred Clay, a revelation that made Brodie smile. Later, Derrick noted, the group became furtive, proving he'd soon destroy their undeserved popularity.

That turned out to be his last pronouncement as the next report was Kyle Duffield's scrawled summary of finding Derrick's body. Kyle didn't record any interviews with the local heroes, although that wasn't necessarily suspicious, as Kyle's records were so brief; his year in office had generated less paper than Derrick produced every week.

Having gained all the information he could from the records, Brodie began his own investigation by heading to the old depot. He started at the spot where he thought he'd first seen the devil's marshal.

On the rise he found a patch of darker ground that in the night he could have mistaken for a man's form. Feeling more relaxed, he searched until he found an area of flattened ground along with some footprints.

He presumed this was where Kyle had found Malachi's body. But as

Malachi had been dirty, it was likely he and the others had been held captive elsewhere, suffocated, and then dumped here.

He examined the warehouse where the witnesses had met, but it was empty, as were the other warehouses. As he didn't trust Kyle's report that Levander had gone into hiding, he headed on to Levander's house.

Levander wasn't there, although he found tracks trailing away, which he followed to the town cemetery.

He clambered over the picket fence and sought out Derrick Shelby's grave, but before he found it, a feeling that he was being watched made him uncomfortable. He turned, but the nearby land was flat and only a timber building in the corner of the plot marred his view.

He went to the building and pushed open the only door. When his eyes became accustomed to the gloom, he winced.

Set out in the middle of the single

room was a rolled up blanket, inside of which lay Levander Bass. He was covered up with only his gagged face visible, and his form was so still, Brodie was unsure if he was dead or alive.

He moved across the room to stand over Levander. Fear had widened Levander's eyes, but they softened when he saw who had arrived.

'You fine?' Brodie asked, slipping the gag away.

'I am now,' Levander said with a voice that was gruff with concern.

Levander shook himself while straining, showing he was trapped in the blanket. So Brodie knelt and tried to work out how he could free him.

'Who did this?' he asked.

'You know. The dead are walking again . . . ' Levander trailed off. With frantic eye movement, he looked pointedly over Brodie's shoulder.

Brodie looked behind him to see that a man stood in the open doorway. He was dressed in black and dangling from his hand was a knife, the long, cruel blade glinting in the light coming from outside.

That didn't shock Brodie as much as the man's face. The first time he'd tussled with the devil's marshal, he'd caught only a glimpse of it and he'd seen only skin.

This time the man had drawn down the brim of his hat and beneath it Brodie could see only blank skin, as if he didn't have a face at all. Still bemused by the sight, Brodie inched his hand towards his six-shooter, and that encouraged the man to break into a run, heading straight for him.

Abandoning caution, Brodie hurled his hand to his gun. He'd yet to draw when his opponent covered the four paces to loom over him. Brodie backed away while standing up, giving him time to slip his gun from its holster.

With his forearm the man batted Brodie's gun hand aside and then drove onwards to pin him against the wall. The back of Brodie's gun hand hit the wall and his assailant followed up by grabbing his wrist and slamming it against the wall for a second time.

Pain shot across Brodie's knuckles causing the gun to fall from his grasp. His assailant took advantage by swinging up the knife and jabbing it into the underside of Brodie's chin. The blade was sharp and Brodie felt only a nick, but that was followed by warmth running down his neck.

He raised himself and looked at his assailant's blank face. Despite his desperate situation, the sight made him sigh with relief.

At close quarters, he saw that the man wore a blank mask with only thin slits for his eyes that in the gloom were just dark pits. Faced with an impenetrable adversary, Brodie gulped to moisten his dry throat and then spoke from the corner of his mouth without moving his jaw.

'You're the faceless, silent spectre, but you're no dead man walking. So what would you look like if you weren't afraid of being recognized, and what would you say if you were prepared to talk?' The man didn't react, making Brodie glance at his covered mouth. 'Or perhaps you can't talk and so you do your talking in another way.'

The man appeared to accept this viewpoint by inclining his head. He lowered the knife letting Brodie rock back down on to his heels.

The moment he'd regained his balance, Brodie used what might be his only chance to fight back by throwing his free hand to the man's wrist. The man didn't seek to raise the knife any higher, but he resisted and stopped Brodie from lowering it.

They strained, and the impasse dragged on until, with Brodie making no headway, he sought an alternate way to free himself. He braced his back against the wall and pushed off, seeking to slip by the devil's marshal.

To his surprise his opponent didn't try to stop him and he was able to barge past him while tearing his wrist away from the man's grip.

He enjoyed a moment of freedom when he faced the door, but then his assailant grabbed the back of his neck and shoved him down. The devil's marshal was strong and he bent him over easily.

Then the man turned him to the side wall and ran him at it. Brodie had enough time to raise an arm before his face, but that didn't cushion the blow and his forehead collided with the wall with a sickening thud.

Unable to control his movements Brodie slumped to his knees, only for his assailant to knock his head against the wall again. Whether or not he hit him for a third time Brodie couldn't tell as the next he knew he was lying in the corner with his head propped up against the wall.

The room appeared to be swaying and he needed several long breaths before he regained his composure. Then he tried to get up, but he couldn't move and, when he looked down, he saw that he was now bound with ropes inside the blanket in which Levander had been trapped.

Brodie squirmed, rolling himself on to his side and away from the wall. The effort made nausea burn his throat and so he had to lay his cheek on the ground and rest.

His new position let him see Levander lying in the opposite corner; he too was encased in ropes. Brodie stayed still while he fought back the nausea. He heard nothing and so he risked calling out to Levander.

'Is he still around?' he asked with a hushed whisper.

Levander acknowledged he'd heard him by shifting his weight, but he didn't reply and, when a footfall sounded outside, Brodie saw why. The devil's marshal stepped into the doorway where he considered Brodie's bound form with his enforced blank expression before moving to Levander.

He dragged him into the centre of the room, seemingly positioning him so that Brodie could see the length of his body with his head closest to him. The man moved out of sight before returning with his knife held in one hand and a metal object clutched in the other.

He stood over Levander with one foot on either side of his head and with his back to Brodie, making sure Levander saw what was in his hands. A moment before the devil's marshal knelt down, Brodie worked out what he planned to do, leaving him with no option other than to close his eyes.

Levander uttered a pitiful, murmured plea to be left alone. Then the sound converted into a shriek that grew in volume until it stopped with a cough and then a choking sound.

An ominous silence followed and even though Brodie knew he'd regret it, he edged open an eye. The assault was progressing in the way he'd feared.

The devil's marshal had used a clamp to draw the tip of Levander's tongue out beyond his lips for several inches. Then he thrust the knife into

Levander's mouth. Brodie closed his eyes so he only had to listen to the screams that became more guttural until they ended with a gurgle.

A thud and then a scraping sound followed. When Brodie opened his eyes a fraction, it was to see Levander being dragged away, leaving a snail's trail of blood on the ground.

The door closed and then he could only listen to the devil's marshal move Levander around. Presently, he heard receding hoof beats, leaving him to lie on his back and contemplate his likely fate.

9

As Brodie didn't know when the devil's marshal would return, he devoted his energies to moving, snake-like, across the floor to the door.

This took him fifteen minutes, as after every few movements he had to stop to get his breath back and rest his strained muscles. He saw nothing in the bare room he could use to free himself and he reckoned that if he kept moving until sunup, he would struggle to get even a dozen yards away from the cemetery.

As it turned out, the closed door was an insurmountable obstacle.

He planted his encased feet against the door and tried rocking it open. Then he swung round and nudged it with his chin, to no avail.

Once he'd accepted he couldn't free himself, the afternoon dragged on until, with the light dimming, hoof beats approached.

Brodie tried to keep his fear at bay as he listened to the rider draw up and dismount. He held on to the hope that the devil's marshal had targeted specific men and had no reason to kill him.

Even so, he exhaled with a relieved sigh when the door edged open and Deputy Farlow peered down at him, his surprised expression turning to a delighted one when he noted Brodie's predicament.

'So while I was looking everywhere for Levander,' Erskine said with a sarcastic gleam in his eye, 'you were resting up out here.'

'How did you find me?' Brodie asked after the deputy had stopped gloating and had started to free him.

'My former boss saw you heading this way earlier,' Erskine said, 'so I retraced your movements.'

His neutral tone acknowledged that he knew how Brodie would react to this information, and so Brodie limited himself to a scowl.

When they headed back to town, Brodie told him what had happened to Levander. Erskine said nothing, but when they arrived back at the law office, he made him a coffee.

'At least four men dead,' Brodie said wearily between sips from his steaming mug. 'Has Hamilton ever had as bad a time as this?'

'No, but then again you've never been the marshal here before. You'll never replace Kyle. He looked for outlaws, not ghosts.'

'The man who kidnapped Levander was no ghost.'

'Except nobody else has seen this spectre who haunts the depot and now the cemetery. I reckon you invented that story to cover up the fact your sister's free and the dead and the missing are men who testified against her.' Erskine chuckled when Brodie frowned. 'But you have only another day to sort this out and then it'll be the new marshal's responsibility.'

'Don't look so pleased with yourself. Kyle didn't think you good enough to be marshal, so I doubt anyone else will.'

Erskine supped his coffee, his pensive expression promising that any attempt Brodie made to explain what he'd seen and what he suspected would receive sarcasm and veiled accusations. Brodie wasn't in the mood to trade words and so, when he finished his coffee, he headed back to the hotel.

To his surprise, Lucinda and Genevieve were in his room. They were taking advantage of the view his window afforded, although watching the news get passed around about Malachi's death and Levander's fate had made them as concerned as he was.

He tried to put their minds at rest, but he didn't have the energy to talk for long and he had to excuse himself with a request for hot water to remove the stiffness created by his prolonged incarceration.

Genevieve saw to his needs, seemingly pleased to have a task to take her mind off the situation. In a cluttered room in which she'd dumped what appeared to be unwanted items, she filled a tub with steaming, soapy water before leaving him, but he didn't enjoy his bath for long.

When he lay back in the water to run his gaze over the detritus, he flinched upright.

The devil's marshal was watching him from the shadows.

He emerged from the tub, splashing water everywhere as he looked for his gun until his spooked senses overcame his instincts and let him work out what he'd really seen. He looked again at the corner and saw that what he'd taken for a man's form was in fact a coat resting on a hook while a mask dangled from a higher hook.

Still concerned, he headed to the corner where he found a table covered with similar, blank masks of the kind the devil's marshal had worn. Feeling pensive, he completed his ablutions quickly and with a mask clutched to his chest, he left.

He wondered if he should question Genevieve tonight, but as it turned out, she was still in his room. While Lucinda had retired for the night, Genevieve was sitting at the window looking at a group of men, who had gathered outside the Sundown to chat.

'I hope you don't mind me waiting in here,' she said. 'I reckon I've calmed your sister down, but I'd now like you to do the same for me.'

'I'm not sure I can do that,' he said, joining her at the window. 'I didn't want to get Lucinda's hopes up, but I was attacked by the man who must have killed Archibald Harper, along with Bartholomew and Malachi, and now possibly Levander Bass. I'll have to catch him to prove her innocence, but then, hopefully, he might resolve what happened to your husband, too.'

Genevieve jutted her jaw as she considered this information before shaking her head. She cast her eyes downwards.

'If you tell me that man is Derrick's spectre, you will leave here tonight.'

'He's not his spectre. This man assaulted me, shot at me, and tied me up. He's real, but until others see him and survive to tell the tale, I guess I'll have to accept that some people will try to discredit my investigation by saying I'm hunting for a ghost.'

She looked shamefaced, suggesting his guess had been right, that Kyle had spoken to her and poured scorn on his theory. Appearing flustered, her gaze alighted on the mask.

'Why did you take that?'

He sat facing her. 'I hoped you'd tell me where it came from.'

'The previous owner left them,' she said without concern. 'The dances he held often involved dressing up, which reminds me that I've been wondering if I can help the situation in town, provided it's not become too out of control.'

'I'd welcome any suggestions,' Brodie said wearily.

'I've been thinking about your idea of holding a dance again. Tomorrow is Friday, and that's a year and a week since my husband died. I promised I'd move on after a year, but if I have a future here, I won't have to fulfil that promise. Holding a successful dance could be my last chance to stay.'

Her heartfelt speech made him give her suggestion serious thought. While he fingered the mask.

His task was the seemingly impossible one of catching a man he knew to be real, but who everyone else thought a spectre. The devil's marshal was determined to keep his anonymity and he was always one step ahead of him.

Worse, he had only one full day to arrest him before Kyle's parting gift put him in a cell.

To catch him, he had to set a trap that would entice him out of hiding. Although he'd never seen the face of the devil's marshal, he had seen him wearing a mask and so, if he saw him again, he'd probably recognize him from his size and build.

'With bodies mounting up every day, a social event could be as sensible as smoking a cigar while sitting on a powder keg,' he said. He waited until she frowned and then took her hand. 'But on the other hand, the situation can't get no worse and so music and dancing and good cheer might be what we all need. Hold that dance, with my blessing.'

She smiled and then looked aloft with her eyes bright, seemingly planning or perhaps recalling the past dances. She didn't try to remove her hand from his and Brodie didn't complain.

'Thank you.'

'Except I have one condition.' He gestured with the mask. 'It'll be a masked dance. Everyone must wear one of these and you'll make sure everyone in town knows that.'

'Why?'

He shrugged. 'If everyone remains anonymous, it might reduce arguments and tensions.'

She looked at him oddly, but he didn't detect that she was concerned because she knew the devil's marshal had worn a mask and that Brodie was throwing down a challenge for him to attend.

'Lucinda liked the idea, too. We'll work out the arrangements tomorrow. It'll give her something else to think about.' She gave him a worried look. 'I didn't want to mention it when she was here, but we started sitting together because I'd seen a man loitering around outside. I reckon he was looking for her.'

Brodie frowned. 'That sounds like Chauncey Spurlock. I'll keep an eye on him. I don't want her to be worried, or you.'

She mustered a nod, and yet still she didn't move her hand away. Then, with a sudden movement, as if she'd only just noticed where her hand was, she looked at it.

With a far-away look in her eyes, she stroked the back his hand. Her touch was light and in response Brodie gently squeezed her other hand, which made her turn it over and entwine her fingers in his.

They sat like that for a while, both leaning forward, her two hands clasping his while his right hand that held the mask dangled awkwardly. He became self-conscious and, so emboldened, he placed the mask on his lap and then reached up to her to finger a lock of dangling hair.

She rubbed her cheek against the back of his hand making his heart thud. Then she closed her eyes and a satisfied purr escaped her lips.

Almost as if that sound had broken the spell, she gulped and then leapt to her feet, tearing her hands away from his grip before smoothing down her skirt with flustered movements.

'I have to go,' she said in a louder

voice than necessary.

'If you get worried again,' Brodie said with a smile, 'you know where I am.'

She considered him with a wide-eyed look, almost akin to horror.

'I do, and that's the problem.'

She backed away and walked into the chair, toppling it with a clatter. She bent to right it, thought better of making the attempt, and then turned and tripped over a leg, making her stumble.

She stood stiff-backed, taking deep breaths. Then she walked across the room. She didn't look back, although when she'd closed the door, he didn't hear footsteps in the corridor.

Brodie headed to the door, resolving that if he heard her breathing on the other side of the door, he'd open it. He heard nothing, but he still stood there for five minutes before he looked outside.

The corridor was empty, but she'd dropped a lace kerchief outside his door and her shoes lay by the wall. They were set askew as if she'd walked out of them so that she could move away quietly.

That sight told Brodie that no matter how tired he was, he'd struggle to sleep tonight.

10

When Brodie awoke for his last full day as a lawman, he still felt as confused about his brief interlude with Genevieve as he had been the night before.

He reckoned she would probably still be confused and need time to think, and might appreciate not having to see him alone at breakfast. So he went in search of his sister.

Lucinda had a room at the back of the hotel where her presence stood the best chance of going undetected. He walked around the corridors, but then heard someone moving around nearby and so he stopped at the top of the stairs.

When he peered over the bannister, he heard Genevieve clinking cutlery in the dining room, confirming that the earlier sound had come from upstairs. Feeling concerned, he moved on quietly to Lucinda's room and rapped on the door.

'Come in,' Lucinda said, her voice light and with a delighted giggle in her tone.

Pleased that his sister had overcome her fears overnight, he went in to find she was lying on the bedspread. She presented a sight he knew he'd struggle to forget, no matter how hard he tried.

'It's me!' he gasped, slapping his hands over his eyes and turning away.

A worried squeal sounded followed by Lucinda leaping off the bed and then wrestling herself into her gown.

'You caught me sleeping,' she blurted out.

'I've never seen anyone sleeping in that position,' Brodie spluttered. He thrust out a hand, searching for the door while keeping his eyes clamped tightly shut.

He struggled to find the door and so he cranked open an eye to be confronted by a second, equally worrying sight. Chauncey Spurlock was about to enter the room.

Brodie slapped a hand against Chauncey's chest and shoved him out into the corridor.

'What are you doing?' Chauncey muttered.

'A woman's in there and she's in no state to see anyone.'

Chauncey stood his ground and gave Brodie a long look that made him piece together the situation with a groan.

'I know your sister's in there,' Chauncey said around a smile, 'and I'm sure she'd have much preferred to see me coming in instead of you.'

'I picked up on that the moment I went in.' Brodie set his hands on his hips. 'How long has this been going on?'

Chauncey didn't answer but instead looked over Brodie's shoulder at Lucinda.

'That's our concern only,' she called, coming up to his shoulder, 'and I'd welcome you leaving us alone now.'

'I can't,' Brodie said. 'Chauncey has

business with me downstairs.'

'The time's long passed when you could order men to stay away from me.'

Brodie had done that only when, as youngsters, he'd chaperoned her at dances, but he accepted her demand with a nod.

'You're right, except I don't intend to warn him off. I'm about to offer him a job.' He nudged Chauncey's shoulder and then pointed downstairs. 'Say goodbye to my sister and then meet me in the dining room in five minutes.'

As it turned out, Chauncey took fifteen minutes and then excused himself to take food up to Lucinda. When he returned, he considered Brodie with his usual smirk.

'What job,' Chauncey asked, 'can you offer a man who's already proved he's a better manhunter than you are?'

'We're still even. But I've decided I need to appoint a second deputy to help me resolve this current crisis. I need someone who is capable and who I can trust.' He waited until Chauncey shook his head before continuing. 'Until I find that man, you'll do.'

'You must be desperate to stop me beating your tally, but I have to decline. I have better and more profitable things to do.'

Chauncey turned away, but Brodie lunged for his arm. He held him tightly and then got up to face him.

'How do you know Lucinda?'

Chauncey turned and considered Brodie's hand until he removed it.

'Until last night, I didn't. I was searching for Phineas Moon and a hotel hardly anyone uses felt like a place he'd hide in, but I came across your sister. She wasn't keen on going back to jail.'

Chauncey licked his lips while searching Brodie's eyes for his reaction. Brodie looked away and moved as if to sit back down before, with a sudden change of intention, he hurled a backhanded blow at Chauncey's face.

Chauncey was prepared for his move. With a casual gesture he raised a hand to catch Brodie's fist and then tried to lever his hand down, but Brodie counteracted by holding his arm firm.

For long moments they strained, with neither man getting the upper hand.

'You're stronger than you look,' Brodie said. 'You'll need that strength when you're my deputy.'

'I refuse and, when I say that, I mean it. Unlike your sister, who only needed a little persuasion,' Chauncey chuckled. 'Although by the morning she was eager for more, as you saw.'

'You still have a lot to learn. Trying to anger a man who's already angry is wasted effort.'

Brodie strained a mite harder, forcing Chauncey to counter his move. Then Brodie relaxed and let his arm rock down making Chauncey double over. He slapped his free hand on the back of Chauncey's jacket and, while he was still unbalanced, he turned him towards his table and ran him at it.

Chauncey couldn't avoid folding over the table before he and the table tipped over to land with a thud on the floor amidst scattered cutlery and uneaten food. Calmly, Brodie went round the table and hunkered down in front of him.

Chauncey rescued his hat before glaring at Brodie.

'I'm looking for Phineas Moon,' he said. 'He's all I want and then I move on.'

'I can't let you do that after you violated a woman who — '

'She was willing!'

'When I tell the story, she won't be. As a lawman, I'll be believed and you know how trials go in this town.'

Chauncey uttered an exasperated screech.

'All right! I'll accept, just to stop you talking.' Chauncey held out a hand and Brodie drew him to his feet. 'But remember, the longer I stay here, the longer I'll be with your sister.'

'I'm pleased.' Brodie slapped Chauncey on the back. 'Given more time, she might make you into a decent man.'

Despite Brodie's concerns about what the day would bring, his worst fears didn't materialize.

The news of Levander's disappearance had depressed the townsfolk, but his body hadn't yet turned up and nobody else had gone missing overnight. So while Deputy Farlow patrolled around town, Brodie and Chauncey headed out to the old depot.

They moved across the site cautiously, covering each other as they explored the area around the warehouses and then inside each building. They found no sign of anyone having returned since the day before and so they moved on to the cemetery, where they searched for tracks.

They found an interesting and recent set heading away from town, although to their irritation these tracks skirted around the town and then returned. Long before they reached Hamilton, the tracks merged in with others leading to the two men riding around fruitlessly for an hour before they admitted defeat.

'It looks,' Brodie said, 'as if we followed the wrong person.'

'Either that, or your spectre has vanished again,' Chauncey said with a grin before leaning towards him. 'I heard the rumour that your only suspect is a ghost.'

'Do you believe that rumour?'

By way of an answer, Chauncey turned away and rode on. He said nothing, but Brodie soon saw that he was heading to Wilfred Clay's house, an observation that made him sigh with relief as his new deputy showed he thought logically.

When they drew up outside the house, the quiet scene reminded Brodie of the last time he'd been there. So when gunfire cracked, for a moment he wondered if his memory was playing tricks on him. When Chauncey quickly leapt down from his horse, however, he shook off his surprise.

He joined Chauncey and both men glanced around before nodding towards the scrub. A second shot tore out, this time slicing into the ground between the two men and so without comment, they sought cover.

They hurried to the house and lay down on their chests amidst the debris that still littered the porch. Brodie rested his gun hand on a rusted bucket while Chauncey thrust his arms out before him and held his gun two-handed.

From the undergrowth three rapid shots tore out, splattering along the wall at a level that would have hit them if they'd been standing up.

'The shooter's just trying to keep us down,' Chauncey said.

'Or he's moved further away,' Brodie said.

Brodie knelt and, when that didn't attract gunfire, he got to his feet. Cautiously he moved off the porch and then glanced over his shoulder at Chauncey, who gestured ahead with a bemused look that said if he wanted to risk his life on a hunch, he wouldn't join him.

Brodie moved on, gaining in confidence as he failed to attract retaliation. The moment he slipped into the scrub he sped to a trot and only slowed when he reached the area where he reckoned the shooter had been.

In the distance hoof beats sounded and so he craned his neck. A rider was fleeing and although he was two hundred yards away, Brodie recognized the dark form of the devil's marshal.

He noted the rider's direction and then headed back through the scrub. When he emerged into clear space, Chauncey was approaching from the back of the house, and he was sporting a concerned expression.

'Someone's been living in the house,' he said. 'And I'd guess we disturbed him.'

Chauncey beckoned Brodie to follow him and he led him to a large and recently dug hole that put Brodie in mind of a grave.

With their moods sober, they searched the surrounding scrub until Chauncey came across Levander's body. Levander lay on his back with his mouth wide open, looking as frightened as the others had done when they'd been found.

Having confirmed where the devil's marshal had holed up while he'd killed the witnesses, they left the house and followed his tracks. Even though Brodie knew the direction their quarry had taken, they soon lost his trail, leaving the two experienced man-hunters to stop and glare at each other in exasperation.

'The hardest men to track down,' Brodie said, 'are the men who track down other men.'

Chauncey nodded. 'It doesn't look as if either of us will get our eleventh quarry today.'

With the discovery of Levander's body and their failure to find the devil's marshal depressing both men, in the late afternoon they returned to town. Brodie ordered his deputies to spend the remainder of the afternoon patrolling and ensuring that news of Levander's death didn't increase tensions, before they reported for guard duty at the dance.

He returned to Derrick Shelby's reports. With only limited time now available, he figured his best hope was to find answers in the past, as the former marshal appeared to be his most reliable source of information.

With every person who had been connected to the train raid, and then Derrick Shelby's murder, being dead, he looked for new names. There were none.

That discovery forced him to try a different approach. When he'd first arrived in town, he'd heard the rumour that Phineas Moon had led the raiders who had attacked the train.

Although Derrick believed there had never been a raid, since his escape Chauncey reckoned Phineas hadn't strayed far from Hamilton, and so he looked for his name.

He couldn't find that, either. This fact made Brodie tap his forehead on his desk with frustration until the thought came that maybe Derrick's very failure to mention Phineas could explain the situation.

Although he wasn't sure what he was looking for, he sought out other reports that had come in on crimes in other counties. He found numerous references to Phineas; he'd committed a variety of crimes, with raids and robberies being his most frequent misdemeanours, but he was less skilled at getting away afterwards.

He'd been caught ten times, usually soon after the crime, but he made up for his lack of skill in staying undetected by his expertise in escaping.

The breakout from the cage in which Lucinda had been held was the tenth time he'd escaped justice and, even without Brodie's intervention, he'd got hold of a key and clearly had a plan in mind.

Despite his dubious past and the rumours about his involvement in the raid, Derrick had never once mentioned him as a suspect. So either the confident Derrick had been right to ignore him, or later someone had removed all references to him from the reports.

Based on what Brodie had seen since arriving in Hamilton that could be only one man.

'Kyle Duffield,' he muttered to himself.

He had tried to avoid jumping to that conclusion, but now he couldn't escape the fact that unless Derrick really had returned from beyond the grave, Kyle was the only one left who could be the devil's marshal.

He went to the door, but before he could leave Erskine returned.

'Chauncey and me have given up for the day,' the deputy reported.

'You'll give up for the day when I say so.'

Erskine set his hands on his hips. 'We give up when the town's peaceful, which it is. I've even heard some enthusiasm for tonight's dance.'

Erskine tapped a foot on floor rhythmically suggesting what was on his mind.

'If you want to dance the night away, we'll share guard duty.' Brodie waited until Erskine provided a stern nod before pointing to the far end of town. 'But only after you've finished your last duty of the day. We need to talk to Kyle Duffield.'

'I can do both at the same time. I've just met Kyle. He's all dressed up in his best clothes and he's heading to the Shelby Hotel ready to dance the night away, too.'

Brodie frowned. 'Then I hope he won't be disappointed when I step on his toes.'

11

The townsfolk were responding to the dance with more enthusiasm than Genevieve could have hoped for.

Two dozen people were milling around outside the hotel. Apparently, the owner of the Four Aces had closed the saloon for the night so he could attend and so several saloon girls were amongst the gathering, a sight that was encouraging more men to gravitate towards the hotel.

The surprises didn't end there. When Brodie and Erskine went inside, they found Chauncey was already going into the main room. He was clutching a fiddle in one hand and a banjo in the other.

'Do you know what those are used for?' Erskine said.

'I'm not only the most handsome lawman in town,' Chauncey said. He placed the fiddle on the floor and then plucked a banjo string producing a surprisingly tuneful sound. 'I'm also the best musician.'

Erskine snorted. 'You're not even the most handsome deputy in town.'

'And you're not the best banjo player in town, either,' Brodie said, remembering how Lucinda had played well when she was younger.

'I know,' Chauncey said, 'so I'll be strumming the fiddle tonight.'

Chauncey gave Brodie a significant look. When Brodie caught on to his meaning, he bade Erskine take the musical instruments into the main room and then drew Chauncey aside.

'You can't let Lucinda play.'

'She was bored hiding upstairs, and planning tonight with Genevieve made her eager to come downstairs and play.' He lowered his voice. 'And I haven't forgotten my duties. I'll keep an eye out for your masked spectre from the front of the room.'

Chauncey waited until Brodie nodded

and then pointed at a table near the door. Brodie smiled when he saw that Genevieve had set out the masks on the table, and he got an early opportunity to test if his trap had worked when Kyle emerged from the main room with Erskine.

He held out a mask to Kyle. 'We're all to wear one of these.'

Kyle took the mask and fingered it while sporting a bemused smile. Then he slipped it on and turned to each of them.

'How do I look?' he asked.

Brodie judged he was broadly of the same build as the devil's marshal, but his deputies nodded approvingly.

'Like a man in disguise,' Erskine said as he slipped into a mask of his own.

Kyle shrugged and then headed back into the main room. Brodie was unsure if this development had perturbed Kyle, but when others arrived and started queuing up for masks, he ordered Erskine to stay by the door and watch out for anyone acting suspiciously while he followed Kyle.

'I didn't expect you'd come here tonight,' Brodie said when he'd joined Kyle at a table in the corner.

'I'm leaving tomorrow,' Kyle said with a catch in his throat. 'So I had to come.'

Brodie slipped into his own mask and moved it around until he could see through the slits.

'Why?'

'To find out the truth.' Kyle raised a hand to show Brodie it was shaking. 'Which is why I'm so nervous, but not so nervous that I couldn't write a letter to the mayor. It'll be on his desk first thing tomorrow.'

Brodie shrugged. If guilt was causing Kyle's worried demeanour, he couldn't see why he'd admit he was nervous.

'I reckon this matter will be resolved in the next few hours.' Brodie leaned towards Kyle. 'So I'd like to know what you reckon will happen tonight.'

'I don't know, I just don't.' Kyle reached under his mask and dabbed at his cheeks with a kerchief, his attitude giving Brodie the impression he wasn't referring to the devil's marshal. 'I've waited a year for this night and everything is still in the balance.'

Feeling confused about what Kyle meant, it was now Brodie's turn to reach under his mask to rub his brow, but he put aside his confusion when the first woman to enter the room arrived.

Lucinda had attached her mask to her face with multiple ties and she wore baggy male clothing that should further help her to avoid casual attention. She glanced in Brodie's direction only briefly showing that his disguise was a good one before Chauncey drew her away to the front of the room. There, they busied themselves with their musical instruments.

Brodie was pleased to see Chauncey treat her with respect and so, after watching them for a while, he relaxed enough to watch the other patrons troop inside.

The masks appeared to be a good

idea as everyone was laughing at the effect they created, but Brodie didn't let the good cheer distract him from examining each person as they entered.

Over the next ten minutes, thirty people came in. They were mostly men and, like Kyle, many of them were the same size and build as the devil's marshal, although none of them acted suspiciously.

Without fanfare, Chauncey and Lucinda launched into a jaunty tune that encouraged the dancing to start. The women all piled out on to the floor with most of the men moving after them.

The music and pattering feet drew Erskine inside. He leaned on the wall beside the door and looked around until Brodie raised a hand to identify himself.

With a thumbs-up signal, Erskine signified that all was well outside after which he settled back to watch the dancers, tapping the raised sole of his boot against the wall.

'Not tempted to join in?' Brodie asked, leaning towards Kyle.

'I've never danced before,' Kyle said.

'Then why have you . . . ?' Brodie trailed off when another woman came in.

She wore a bright red dress and, despite the mask, he was sure he recognized her, although he couldn't work out where he'd seen her before.

Only when she spoke with Erskine and he pointed out his table did he realize with a gulp that it was Genevieve Shelby and she was wearing non-black clothing for the first time since he'd known her.

Several men moved in on her with invitations to dance, but she breezed past them as she headed to Brodie's table. Brodie was aware of Kyle shuffling anxiously on his chair, but he had eyes only for Genevieve as she walked towards him with a hand held out.

Clearly she'd thought about their brief, intimate moment the previous night and now she'd decided she wanted to follow it up. Now that he thought about it, Brodie realized in a sudden rush that made his palms sweat and his mouth go dry that he wanted to find out where it might lead, too.

He stood up, his hand rising to take hers, only for Kyle to barge in front of him and grab her hand first. Brodie slapped Kyle's shoulder and tried to move him aside, but Kyle didn't react to his action and instead bowed to Genevieve.

She returned the bow and then Kyle led her back to the dance floor. To Brodie's irritation, Genevieve didn't object.

Then, with a sinking feeling that made him slump back on to his chair, Brodie connected several things he'd seen and heard over the last few days but which he hadn't understood at the time.

Kyle had feelings for Genevieve and he had been pestering her. She had rebuffed his advances as she was still in mourning, but she'd promised him that she'd consider the matter seriously once a year had passed since Derrick's death.

With that time now up, Kyle had resigned as town marshal so that he could leave town, either with Genevieve or without her. She had promised him she'd decide today and, from her choice of clothing and her actions, she'd clearly decided in Kyle's favour.

With a hand propping up his head, Brodie watched them whirl and pivot. Kyle lumbered around like a new-born calf that had yet to work out why it'd been given legs, while she was dainty on her feet. Then again, she needed to be to avoid Kyle's heavy-footed attempt at dancing, but both of them appeared happy.

Three tunes later, they were still on the floor and even though Kyle's dancing hadn't improved, Genevieve was showing no sign of wanting to dance with anyone else.

With a long sigh, Brodie got to his

feet and plodded to the door to join Erskine, deciding that carrying out his duties would take his mind off his disappointment.

'You get the answers you wanted from him?' Erskine asked.

'I haven't probed him deeply yet. I'd hoped he'd incriminate himself, but all he had on his mind was Genevieve.'

'I can't blame him. And it's about time we changed duties. I've been standing guard all night and your ghost hasn't showed up yet.'

Brodie slapped him on the back. 'Go and dance, but if you don't move your feet better than Kyle's doing, you're back on guard duty.'

Erskine snorted a laugh before he moved off into the throng of dancers where he quickly gained a partner. Brodie watched him, as that was less irritating than watching Kyle and Genevieve.

Thankfully, the dancers didn't look at Lucinda, so he headed to the front door. Nobody else was gravitating towards the hotel and so he checked on the rest of the hotel before he returned to the main room where, for the next half-hour, he loitered at the door.

He considered each dancer. He judged that a dozen men resembled the devil's marshal, although none was more distinctive than the rest.

When yet another fast dance started, Kyle and Genevieve joined him at the door. Genevieve removed her shoes to rub her feet while Kyle leaned back against the wall with a sigh of relief. As Genevieve was still swaying to the music, Kyle leaned towards him.

'Will you dance with her now?' he asked between gasps for air. 'I need a rest and a drink.'

'I'm watching the door.' Brodie took a deep breath. 'And it seems that tonight belongs to you two.'

'It does, so I don't want anyone else butting in and dancing with her, but she'll be safe with you.' Kyle patted his arm. 'I'll watch the door.'

Brodie was grateful he was wearing a

mask, as he couldn't stop himself scowling. But he accepted Kyle's offer with good grace and a bow, as did Genevieve, and so he led her out on to the dance floor where they started with reels.

'You dance well,' Genevieve said when they came close.

'It's been a while,' Brodie said, 'but I can still remember what I used to do.'

Their movements kept them apart for a minute, but when they were next close, she leaned in to whisper hoarsely in his ear, her voice muffled by the mask.

'All day I've wanted to speak to you about last night.'

'So have I.'

'Would it help if I told you I wanted to dance with you first tonight?' She swayed away and then swayed back. 'But Kyle has waited for so long and I had promised to dance with him first.'

'It helps,' Brodie gulped, 'but I guess it doesn't matter who you dance with first. All that matters is who you dance with last.'

As they moved apart, she laughed lightly and so Brodie held his breath in anticipation of what she'd say the next time they came close. But he didn't get to hear it, as she then rocked away from him with a light-footed step and with an arm thrust out, which encouraged another dancer to take her hand.

With a deft manoeuvre the man swung her away leaving her to cast Brodie an apologetic shrug before she began dancing with her new partner.

Brodie was minded to reclaim her hand, but in his younger days he'd seen fights break out over such matters and he didn't want to spoil the evening's good-natured mood.

He danced on his own while again examining the dancers. He wondered if one of them had taken the bait and walked into his trap until, feeling self-conscious, he headed back to the doorway. Kyle intercepted him.

'I told you to stay with her,' he muttered.

'I didn't get a chance to complain,' Brodie said. He glanced at Genevieve and confirmed she looked content. 'And I left you to guard the door.'

'You guard it. I'm getting her back before this all goes wrong.'

Kyle started to move off, but he stilled when the dancers stomped to a halt and the music died out with a high-pitched screech. Brodie wasn't sure what the problem was until he saw Chauncey put down his fiddle and then stride across the floor towards the door.

He turned to see that a new man had arrived. He was standing in the doorway and, unlike everyone else, he wasn't wearing a mask, letting Brodie identify him as Phineas Moon.

Phineas was armed, and Erskine was already hurrying to join Chauncey. So Brodie moved on.

'Raise those hands,' Chauncey shouted the moment he had a clear view of Phineas.

The dancers between Brodie and the door panicked and blocked Brodie's view. So Brodie had to barge men aside as he tried to reach Phineas first.

'Leave Phineas to me,' he shouted as he emerged into clear space, but his initial fears of a showdown hadn't materialized.

Chauncey had drawn a gun on Phineas while Erskine was working his way closer along the wall. For his part, Phineas had raised a hand in apparent surrender while in the other he clutched a whiskey bottle.

With an inebriated grin on his face, Phineas cast his gaze around the circle of onlookers and then growled at the nearest man. When the man backed away quickly, Phineas roared with laughter and then supped from the bottle, the action almost unbalancing him as he staggered backwards.

He kept his lips wrapped around the bottle until he'd drunk the contents. Then he considered the bottle with disgust and, while clapping his lips together, he hurled it at Erskine, who ducked as it passed several feet overhead.

That action was enough for Brodie and he moved in with his gun aimed at Phineas's chest. Chauncey followed his lead and, as he was several paces closer to Phineas, he reached their target first.

Only when Chauncey was standing before him did Phineas appear to register that he was about to be captured. He moved to flee, but in his drunken state, he failed to find the exit and he staggered away from the doorway knocking into Chauncey, who kept enough presence of mind to disarm him before Phineas moved on.

Brodie then reached him, but Phineas flailed an arm and caught him a glancing blow to the head that knocked him backwards. When Brodie regained his footing, people were spreading out, giving Phineas room.

The three lawmen glanced at each other to co-ordinate their movements and, with them blocking three paths,

Phineas embarked on a snaking walk in the only direction left open to him: the corner of the room.

Lucinda was the only person standing in the corner and, when she saw Phineas advancing on her, she hurried along the wall attempting to reach safety.

Phineas watched her run by with jerking movements that suggested he was struggling to focus until, almost as an afterthought, he lunged at her. From behind, he grasped her short hair before she pulled free, but that action made Chauncey grunt with anger and he hurried towards him.

On the run Chauncey barged into Phineas and both men went down with Chauncey flattening Phineas to the floor. By the time Brodie and Erskine joined them, Chauncey had drawn Phineas's arms up behind him and was kneeling on his back, keeping him secured.

'I can see why this one gets captured easily and often,' Chauncey said.

'He also escapes easily and often,' Brodie said, 'so we take no chances. But you did well . . . '

He trailed off from congratulating Chauncey for his neat arrest when a cry of alarm went up behind him. He swung round to find that nobody was paying them attention as everyone was staring at Lucinda, who was now cowering in the opposite corner of the room.

With a wince, Brodie saw what had concerned them. Phineas had broken the ties on her mask, exposing her face. Although she had covered her face with her arm, the determined movements of everyone else in the room showed that they had worked out who she was.

Then Lucinda ran for the door and, within moments, a stampede of men followed her out into the corridor, discarding their masks as they ran.

'I'll help her,' Chauncey said with a catch in his throat. He leapt to his feet. 'You take care of Phineas.'

As the lawmen threw their masks

aside, Brodie was minded to argue, but Phineas was stirring. As the last of the mob disappeared into the corridor, he signified that Erskine should keep Phineas subdued while he followed Chauncey.

He had yet to set off when he noticed another worrying thing. Kyle was the only man not to chase after Lucinda. He was kneeling in the centre of the room with his hands clutched to his head.

Brodie went to him and even before Kyle spoke, he had worked out what had distressed him.

'Genevieve's gone,' Kyle whined. 'The man who was dancing with her took her away.'

12

'This Phineas Moon,' Erskine said as he stepped back from the cell door, 'isn't anything like what I expected.'

Brodie nodded as, even before Erskine had locked the door, Phineas had slumped down on his cot and begun snoring. He hadn't answered any questions, but he was so drunk Brodie doubted he'd understood them and so only his reputation as a man who was hard to keep prisoner made Brodie look at him with interest.

He wondered if Phineas's inebriation and lack of fighting spirit was a clever subterfuge, but with a shrug he reckoned that didn't matter for now as he was locked up securely.

He decided he'd question him later about the train raid and the devil's marshal, but somehow he doubted

Phineas would help him advance his investigation.

As Erskine had said, Phineas just didn't look and act like the notorious outlaw he'd heard about. He beckoned Erskine to join him in leaving the jailhouse.

In the law office he went to the window and considered the rowdy scene outside, wondering where he could start searching for the two missing women. After Lucinda had fled from the dance, he'd not seen her again and neither had he been able to find Genevieve.

He hadn't seen Chauncey, either, and so, when Kyle headed towards the office, he threw open the door. This increased the noise level and he stood there, considering the milling people.

Unlike the mob that had formed on his first night, this group had no focus. Everyone had gathered to tell each other their version of the events at the dance, but nobody was looking as if they'd organize a systematic search.

This meant that Lucinda was safe for now and hopefully, Chauncey had found her first.

When Kyle reached the door, he dallied to eye the mob. As he did so, with less assurance than the last time he'd faced one, Brodie dragged him inside.

Kyle offered no resistance and he came to a halt standing in the middle of the office with his eyes downcast and two masks clutched to his chest, presumably his and Genevieve's.

'Did you find Genevieve?' Brodie demanded. When Kyle didn't reply, he shook his shoulders and repeated his question.

'That dancer kidnapped her,' Kyle said, his voice small. 'All that time I waited for her and after a few brief moments together, it was over.'

'It's not over. We don't know that she's in trouble. All we know for sure is that she went missing after Lucinda's identity was revealed.'

Kyle raised his head and his confused

expression showed that despite the mob outside, he'd not been aware of this development.

'Which means Lucinda returned to Hamilton,' he said. He tapped a finger against Brodie's chest as he pieced together each part of the situation. 'You hid her, and she was discovered. Then that chaos erupted and when it was over, Genevieve had gone, too.'

He stopped tapping when he failed to link the events in a way that proved Brodie was at fault.

So Brodie took over the accusations, except as he made the points he'd wanted to make all night, he punctuated them by pushing Kyle backwards with firm, flat-handed blows to the chest.

'The devil's marshal kidnapped townsfolk and then killed them. You have the same build as the kidnapper and you claim you found the first three bodies. Now Genevieve's gone and I reckon you know a lot more about that than you've admitted.'

Brodie finished speaking when he'd pinned Kyle against the wall. The former marshal shook his head, but his failure to meet Brodie's eyes confirmed that even if some of Brodie's assumptions were incorrect, his last one was accurate.

'I only wanted Genevieve, nothing more.'

'The man who danced with her could be the devil's marshal, but every name I've come across that's connected to the train raid and Derrick Shelby's death is now dead or locked up in a cell. So that leaves you, the one constant in all this and the only man connected to everything.'

Kyle opened and closed his mouth several times until he settled for a murmured reply.

'You made more sense when you were chasing ghosts.'

Brodie grabbed Kyle's collar and raised him so that he had to look him in the eye.

'I know Derrick Shelby's spectre

hasn't returned, but I'm not the only one who knows that, am I?'

Kyle gulped and when he spoke, his voice was barely audible.

'Maybe the man who took Genevieve doesn't have to be Derrick's spectre.'

Brodie shook him, but Kyle said no more and so in disgust he threw him aside. Kyle stumbled into the desk where he leaned over it, breathing deeply.

'You mean,' Brodie said, 'Derrick feigned his own death and now he's back?'

Kyle stood tall and, with his back to Brodie, faced the door.

'I'll answer your question, but only when I know for sure.'

With that, he set off. His steps were uncertain until he reached the door, where he held on to it for a moment. Then, with a shrug of the shoulders, he adopted a more determined gait and set off outside, leaving Brodie to turn to Erskine.

'I'm still not certain that Phineas

isn't involved in this,' he said. 'So stay here and guard our prisoner, and if Genevieve or Lucinda turn up, protect them.'

Erskine nodded, leaving Brodie to follow Kyle outside. He didn't question Kyle as he scurried along the boardwalk, keeping out of the way of the people who were now filling the road.

It soon became apparent where Kyle was going, making Brodie think for the first time that he'd get answers, even if he balked at the way he'd get them.

Kyle made a detour to his house to collect a spade and a lamp before he headed out of town to the cemetery. As Brodie expected, Kyle went straight to a grave marked for Derrick Shelby where he looked at Brodie, who nodded.

When Kyle started digging, Brodie took the light and leaned on the picket fence that surrounded the site to await the result.

Kyle attacked the ground with vigour, slicing the spade down into the ground and hurling the earth aside. He had burrowed down to his knees when a crunching sound made Kyle stop.

Kyle looked at Brodie for help and so Brodie edged forward, holding the lamp high while averting his face until he knew what Kyle had found inside. When the light fell on the grave, from the corner of his eye, he saw Kyle curl his upper lip.

'I guess,' Kyle said, 'that answers one question.'

Brodie glanced down at the broken coffin lid that revealed a body beneath. His encounters with the devil's marshal had prepared him for the grave being empty and so he wasn't sure what he felt after seeing it occupied.

'Are you sure it's him?' he asked.

Kyle grinned, confirming he'd had the same expectations about what they'd find as Brodie had.

'Before Derrick became a marshal here, he got a broken rib from being shot.'

Kyle took a deep breath and then went to his knees to rummage in the coffin making Brodie, again, avert his face. When Kyle muttered under his breath and then clambered out of the grave, he turned back.

Kyle was clutching a short bone, presumably a rib, and fingering the broken end. His dejected posture removed any doubt that he had lied about the way he could identify Derrick.

'So Marshal Derrick Shelby's dead, after all,' Brodie said in a matter-of-fact tone, 'which means the only possibility is that his spectre has returned.'

Kyle mustered a supportive snort of laughter and then threw the bone back into the grave before he started to refill it. Brodie didn't press him for the explanation he'd promised, as he presumed Kyle was losing himself in the work while he collected his thoughts.

When Kyle had covered up the coffin, he paused for breath and faced Brodie.

'The men who testified against your

sister,' he said with a defeated air, 'killed Derrick Shelby because he was close to proving they'd raided the train themselves.'

Brodie scowled. 'And yet you were Derrick's deputy and you let them get away with it?'

Kyle shovelled more earth into the grave before holding out the spade for Brodie to take over. Brodie passed over the lamp and moved earth for another minute before Kyle spoke again.

'Levander Bass told me they planned to get rid of Derrick, which suited me as I wanted Genevieve, but I made him promise that they wouldn't kill him. Levander accepted my demand without a pause and so I reckoned he already had a plan in mind. He did, and it was a gruesome one that only technically kept the promise.'

Brodie hurled the last few lumps of earth over the grave and then leaned on the spade.

'You said Derrick was shot.'

'I lied. I led him to the old depot

where the others overcame him and took him away. By the time I'd found out what they'd done, it was too late. If I'd told the truth, I'd have been finished, too.'

'What did they do?'

'They trussed him up, cut out his tongue and buried him alive. When everyone attended his funeral, he could have still been alive, trapped down there unable to call out for help until he died from lack of air — '

Kyle broke off when Brodie's anger at this revelation brimmed over and he advanced on him with the spade thrust aloft. Kyle dropped to one knee, his only defence a hand raised before his face, leaving Brodie to loom over him.

Brodie's hand twitched with a desire to deliver the retribution Kyle expected until, with an angry grunt, he hurled the spade aside, ensuring he threw it over the picket fence to remove temptation. Then he dragged Kyle to his feet.

'The only good thing about your story is that the men who conspired to kill Derrick died in the same way: underground, gasping for air and with their tongues sliced out before they were dug up and dumped.'

Brodie turned Kyle to the gate and pushed him on. 'Now, before the same thing happens to Genevieve, take me to the man who killed them.'

When Kyle reached the gate, he turned to Brodie.

'I can't help you,' he said. 'I don't know who this spectre . . . this devil's marshal is.'

'Then think. Someone must know how Derrick died. That person's kidnapped Genevieve and we have to find him before he silences her.'

Kyle shook his head before he moved on.

'She's the first person to be kidnapped who had nothing to do with what happened to Derrick, so she must have been taken to punish me.'

Brodie had no answer to this and so

181

he remained silent as they headed back to town.

Kyle's plodding walk showed that he was thinking about alternatives, so Brodie didn't prompt him as he pondered on who he thought could have taken her.

He was no nearer to an answer when they reached the main drag, which was now deserted, although he could hear a nearby commotion. Without discussion, they sought out the source of the noise.

Brodie wasn't surprised when Kyle caught his attention and pointed along the railtracks towards the old depot.

They hurried out of town and, before they even reached the buildings, Brodie saw that, unlike the previous times he'd been there, dozens of people were crowding around the warehouses. Many were clutching brands, which they held aloft as they jostled to see what was ahead.

By the time Brodie reached the site it became apparent what was holding their attention. Brodie reckoned only one event could have captured so many people's interest and, when he edged forward far enough to see into the warehouse, his worst fears materialized.

Lucinda had been cornered. Chauncey was standing before her, having adopted a protective posture with one hand clutching his gun and the other pointing at his star.

His action had stopped the mob from moving in, but they had formed a tight semicircle that blocked the trapped people's route to the door; their effective noose was tightening.

13

Brodie had seen how the mob had acted on his first night in town when even a hint that he knew Lucinda had swelled their anger, and so he moved forward cautiously.

'Stay back here,' he said to Kyle, but Kyle slapped a hand on his arm and then drew him back.

'I wanted your sister to be guilty to stop me facing up to what I did, but I was wrong. Now it's time for me to make amends.'

'You don't need to do that. You're not a lawman no more.'

'I know.' Kyle provided a thin smile. 'But have you ever considered that I gave you the job because I thought you'd uncover the truth? Now stay back while I talk them down.'

Kyle lingered long enough to receive

a nod from Brodie before he moved on into the mob.

Although his presence would make the situation more fraught, he couldn't let Kyle take all the risks, so he hurried round to the back of the warehouse.

The four buildings were all split into two rooms so he searched for a way into the unoccupied room. Aided by the light from the other side of the warehouse, he located a broken plank in the wall that he was able to lever up before slipping inside.

Ahead was the doorway into the other room where people were pressed tightly together, but they weren't looking his way and so he edged into the shadows to a position where he could see the far end of the room.

Chauncey had drawn his gun and was standing before Lucinda with it aimed at the nearest man, his determined expression promising that he'd shoot the first person to come closer.

Thankfully, that person turned out to be Kyle, who worked his way through the mob to reach clear space where he swung round to face everyone.

'I told you last week that you can't take the law into your own hands. Disperse, people, and — '

'You're not the law here no more,' someone shouted.

'I'm not, but Chauncey is.'

'He was appointed by that woman's brother and if Brodie hasn't got the courage to face us, we're not listening to you.'

This declaration gathered an enthusiastic cheer and then, despite the guns Chauncey and Kyle held on them, the mob took a determined pace towards them.

With neither Chauncey nor Kyle being prepared to shoot into a crowd, they had no choice but to edge away. The semicircle around them tightened until the nearest person was only two paces away from being able to lunge for Lucinda.

The mob's taunts had confirmed his presence would only enflame the situation, but Brodie reckoned he had no choice but to get involved. He hurried on to the internal wall, all the while keeping in the shadows.

Then, with one hand on the wall, he worked his way along it to the doorway. Even his light touch made the wall shake.

When he reached the doorway, the space around the trapped threesome had reduced. The crowd had their backs to him and so, over their heads the tall Chauncey and he were able to look at each other.

Chauncey shook his head and then glanced at his gun, signifying that he wouldn't let them take Lucinda without a fight. With everyone packed so tightly into the warehouse that was sure to result in a bloodbath.

Brodie took a firm grip of the side of the doorway as he prepared to make his presence known, and that action again shook the wall.

As Lucinda and her two protectors were standing before the doorway, the precarious state of the wall made him look up. He saw that the internal wall stopped before the roof and it wasn't supported.

He stepped back for three paces while trying to catch Chauncey's eye to warn him about what he intended to do, but the nearest person was now only a pace away from him.

Suddenly, a gunshot ripped out and several people screamed.

With only moments before Chauncey was forced into retaliating by shooting his way out of trouble, Brodie thrust his shoulder down and ran at the wall.

He had taken two paces when another gunshot sounded. Then he slammed into his target.

The wall tilted and cracked, sending down a flurry of dust as, on the other side of the wall, the hubbub of noise was silenced in an instant.

Footfalls sounded as everyone detected where the danger was coming from, but the wall itself came to rest having adopted only a slight lean.

Two rapid gunshots tore out, although the sound of the creaking wall masked the noise and made it appear as if the firing was coming from some distance away. Brodie stepped back for four paces and then ran at the wall again.

A loud crack sounded as his shoulder slammed into the timbers and his right leg broke through the wall. The resistance from the wood sent him to one knee, but when he tried to extract himself, the wall resolved his problem by tipping over.

He rocked back on his heels as the wall fell away and cries of alarm sounded, but he figured that a few bruises and broken limbs were a better result than the mayhem Chauncey could hand out.

When he gained his feet, the wall had come to rest at an acute angle. One side had been stopped by the outer wall with the far corner four feet off the ground while the other far corner had stopped ten feet from the ground.

As Brodie had hoped, the tilted-over doorway had neatly framed the people he'd hoped to rescue, and they were still standing upright. Scuffling sounded as people scurried to safety beneath the wall while some of those who had been lucky enough to be beneath the doorway dragged others free.

Chauncey and Kyle didn't help with the rescue attempt. They drew Lucinda forward to join Brodie, who pointed at the broken plank in the corner through which he'd entered the warehouse.

'Get her back to town,' he said to Chauncey, 'and hole up with Erskine in the law office. Kyle and me will sort out this situation without further bloodshed.'

'Your biggest problem is the person who was doing the shooting,' Chauncey said. 'He was at the back of the mob, but I couldn't see who he was.'

Chauncey waited until Brodie accepted his explanation with a nod and then moved to drag Lucinda away, but she tore herself free to give Brodie a quick hug.

'Thank you for everything,' she whispered, her earnest gaze making Kyle think she didn't expect to see him again, before she joined Chauncey in hurrying to the corner.

Brodie watched them move away until Chauncey helped Lucinda through the gap.

Then he and Kyle looked under the fallen wall. Several people had been trapped, but the rest who had crouched down to avoid the falling timbers were making no effort to leave.

'Keep moving towards the door,' Brodie shouted. 'We'll get the trapped ones out.'

He hoped his urgent demand would stop anyone from noticing that he had caused the problem and that the subject of their anger had escaped. Sure enough, the faces that turned to him registered only relief.

'We can't leave,' a man shouted from the front. 'Someone's shooting at us from out there.'

Backing up this view, steady gunfire erupted outside. This forced the people in the doorway to scurry backwards, but they could move for only a few paces as they came up against people who were already confined in a small space.

Their movements knocked the wall, making it shake. Then it slipped down for another foot, causing another ripple of panic to spread through the trapped people.

'Who would shoot at these people?' Kyle asked before he frowned as he clearly answered his own question.

'It'd seem,' Brodie said with a heavy heart, 'that the devil's marshal has now decided to take revenge on the whole town.'

'With everyone trapped,' Kyle said unhappily, 'from out there he can pick off everyone with ease.'

Brodie nodded as he grabbed the nearest man to him and shoved him into the doorway.

'Everyone,' he shouted while moving on to grab the next person, 'move this way, and extinguish those torches.'

Torches were dashed against the ground and so Brodie tried to move the next person, but this man resisted. Worse, in the growing darkness, scuffles broke out.

Thankfully, nobody resisted when Kyle started manoeuvring people away and, after he had dragged several people to safety, others caught on to what they were trying to do and more people started heading for the doorway.

Their movement opened up space and let the people at the opposite end move out of danger, but that didn't stop another volley of gunshots peeling out. Someone shouted in pain and people bustled to drag the wounded person to safety.

'Put out all the lights!' Kyle shouted. 'If he can't see us, he can't shoot us.'

Nobody reacted to his demand, however, and the lights at the front of the warehouse continued burning.

With there being at least twenty people between him and the source of the light, Brodie couldn't see who was at fault. He slapped Kyle on the back.

'Keep getting people out. Then direct them to leave out the back and hide in the darkness. I'll go round to the front and deal with the shooter.'

He hurried away to the corner of the building, his action encouraging several others to trail after him now that they could see the escape route. Outside, he stopped to peer into the darkness towards the town.

He couldn't see anyone, giving him hope that Chauncey had got Lucinda to safety without encountering reprisals. Then he turned his attention to the man whose activities had inadvertently given them their chance to flee.

He scurried along to the front corner of the warehouse, where he stopped to consider the scene.

The light from the remaining brands made the other three warehouses stand out in stark relief along with the lower

194

part of the rise, but he couldn't see where the devil's marshal had gone to ground.

He assumed that his inability to see him meant that the devil's marshal was on the rise where he'd first assaulted him. This meant he would have to run over fifty yards of flat ground and then make a steep climb, and along the whole route his progress would be lit up.

He was about to reinforce Kyle's earlier demand that the brands be extinguished when he saw the reason why it hadn't been followed. The area around the door was on fire.

Clearly the falling wall had knocked brands from people's hands and now a fire was burning independently. Already it had started licking at the underside of the leaning wall.

Brodie could see someone lying in the doorway and so he ventured out. He'd covered only two paces when the devil's marshal picked him out.

Splinters kicked from the wall above

his head making him duck and a second gunshot cannoned into the ground at his feet. Brodie put his head down and sprinted for the door, reaching it before the shooter could fire again.

He used the doorframe to swing himself inside and then fell to one knee as he peered out. He hadn't seen where the shots had come from, but they had been wild and he'd presented an easy target, so he assumed the shooter was some distance away, up on the rise.

He loosed off a couple of shots at an area of the rise that provided an uninterrupted view of the warehouse before helping a man who was lying on his side. When he turned him over, he couldn't find a wound so, as the man was still breathing, he assumed the falling wall had knocked him out.

Kyle was getting people out quickly and only the comatose man and four others weren't moving. Brodie grabbed the still man's shoulders and tugged him towards safety.

He'd taken a single step when a loud crack sounded, giving him a moment's warning before the wall crashed down on his back. The blow sent him to his knees and then, when the wall continued pressing down on him, on to his chest.

The sudden rush of air extinguished the dropped brands lying nearby, but he also heard flames crackle as it fuelled the fire around the door.

He flexed his back, finding that he could move relatively freely and so he rolled over and found that the wall was only two feet from his face. He doubted that would give him enough room to drag the comatose man to safety and so he raised his feet to press them against the wall and then pushed.

At first, the rickety wall held and so he strained harder, finding that his feet rose slowly as the wall gave way until, in a burst of splinters and cracked wood, his legs kicked directly upwards.

He clawed at the broken wood, but he didn't have enough freedom of movement to raise himself and for several moments he floundered, with his legs waggling like an upturned beetle and with the wall still pressing down on his chest.

Then, thankfully, hands slapped down on his hips and tugged. With him helping the rescue attempt by pushing backwards with his arms, the helpers dragged him to safety.

When he'd gained his feet, he nodded with relief to his rescuers, who now appeared to be better organized than when he'd left.

He directed them to help the person he'd been trying to aid and then hurried on to help Kyle free the rest of the trapped people. But he couldn't find Kyle inside the warehouse and nobody knew where he'd gone, so he concentrated on encouraging the rest to get out before the fire grew any fiercer.

Unfortunately, the fallen wall had now exposed the main doorway and so the devil's marshal had a clear view of the interior of the warehouse. The helpers kept low as they got to work pulling the last of the injured to safety.

By the time the last person was dragged out, flames were skirting around the entire doorway, lighting up the warehouse, but the expected gunfire from the devil's marshal didn't materialize.

Nobody took any chances and everyone gathered in a corner where they stood less chance of being seen.

Brodie confirmed that nobody had come to any serious harm, finding that the worst injuries were a broken arm, two gunshot nicks and two comatose people.

A dozen people were left in the warehouse, so he allocated two people to look after each injured person.

Then he directed the stragglers across the warehouse, patting each person on the back as they slipped outside through the gap in the corner. The moment the last of them had left, Brodie went in the opposite direction.

He clambered across the fallen wall.

Then, to protect himself from the flickering flames, he hurried through the middle of the doorway with an arm raised before his face.

When the heat at his back lessened, he hunkered down hoping the bright flames behind him would dazzle the shooter.

The firelight was now bright enough to illuminate the whole site and the rise, but still he couldn't see any sign of the devil's marshal. With a stream of townsfolk hurrying away from the back of the warehouse towards town, he had plenty of targets and yet he wasn't taking advantage.

Feeling pensive about his opponent's intentions, he moved on to the nearest warehouse. He pressed himself to the wall to limit the directions from which he could be shot.

The other two buildings were close to the burning section of the warehouse and flames were already licking at their walls. The warehouse he was standing outside was near enough to the fire to leave him in no doubt that the flames would reach it soon, after which the whole depot would burn down before morning.

As the depot was the scene of everything that had gone wrong in Hamilton recently, Brodie wouldn't regret its passing. Before he left, he searched the buildings to check everyone had got away.

The first two warehouses he looked into were empty, but to his surprise, he found Kyle in the final building. He had his back to him as he dragged a rolled-up blanket towards the door.

When Brodie saw that a body was in the blanket, he stopped and levelled his gun on him.

'Stop right there, Kyle,' he shouted.

Kyle flinched and then lowered the blanket to the ground before swinging round.

'I've found Genevieve,' he said, 'and she's unharmed. Help me before the fire claims this building, too.'

His lively tone didn't appear to

register that Brodie had drawn a gun on him and so Brodie moved on, although he didn't holster his gun. When he joined Kyle, he saw that Genevieve had been trussed up in the way that Levander had been secured, with numerous ropes and a gag that Kyle had now slipped away.

'I'm pleased you're all right, too,' she said when she saw him, removing Brodie's last doubts that Kyle had been involved in kidnapping her.

He dropped to one knee to help Kyle remove her bonds.

'And I'm pleased you can still talk,' Brodie said. 'Did you see the face of the man who kidnapped you?'

'No. He kept his mask on and I couldn't work out who he was.'

She cast a worried glance at the room to her side where flames were scooting up the walls, a sight that made Brodie grab her legs.

'We can free her later,' he said. 'For now, we have to get out.'

Kyle nodded and bent down to take

hold of her shoulders, but when he looked up, he flinched and then staggered backwards. Brodie thought he'd been shocked at how close the flames were and so he glanced over his shoulder without too much concern, but that soon changed.

Standing in the doorway was the devil's marshal. He was still wearing his mask and he'd already aimed his gun at them.

14

'Who are you?' Kyle demanded.

The devil's marshal's only answer was to settle his stance.

'You've had plenty of chances to kill Brodie and others,' Kyle persisted, 'but you haven't taken them. So I reckon you want people to know who you are before you kill them.'

The man gave a slight shrug and, as Brodie could see that Kyle was only questioning him to keep him talking, he moved away from him, making it harder for the masked man to shoot them both.

'I'm now the town marshal,' Brodie said, 'and I'll bring to justice anyone who was connected to the train raid and Derrick Shelby's death.'

He waited, but the man didn't reply although he did flick his head up to look at the flames, which were now skittering along the top of the doorway. Kyle chose that moment to throw his hand to his gun.

Brodie reacted a moment later, but the devil's marshal reacted quicker, although to Brodie's surprise he ran to the side of the doorway. Within moments the flames took him out of sight and so both men inside stilled their fire.

'At least,' Kyle said, 'that proves he won't kill us until we know his identity.'

'Then it's good for us that we haven't worked it out yet.'

Kyle flashed a brief smile before pointing at the spreading flames.

Brodie agreed with the sentiment that they shouldn't congratulate themselves yet and so while Kyle covered the door, he sought to free Genevieve. He started with the rope that had been wrapped around the blanket.

Without a knife this was hard to remove and by the time he'd loosened the intricate knot, Kyle was muttering urgently about the spreading fire.

'You have to leave me,' Genevieve said looking Brodie in the eye.

Brodie paused from tearing at the rope to give her an earnest look, but her comment spurred Kyle on. He moved to the side of the doorway that was free of flames and then edged out with his gun thrust forward.

He took only a single step outside before gunfire blasted into the ground before his feet, making him twitch and hurry back inside. He gestured at his foot showing Brodie that the shot had clipped his boot, but he still risked moving forward again, although he took slower steps.

Again a gunshot blasted and again it sliced into the ground at Kyle's feet making him retreat.

'He really doesn't want to kill us,' Kyle said, 'until we know why.'

Kyle then hurried off to look for other ways out of the warehouse, even though it was one of the more robust buildings. With the situation becoming more desperate, Brodie tugged on

Genevieve's rope with frantic gestures.

Just as he was starting to fear he'd never remove the rope, it loosened. He drew the rope away from her body. Then, with a long tug, he slipped it out from under her, thus opening up the blanket.

As he'd feared, this revealed that within the blanket numerous ropes still encased her.

Accordingly, she gave him a sorrowful look that accepted that by the time he'd loosened them all, the warehouse would be completely ablaze. Worse, Kyle returned shaking his head.

'As the door is the only way out of here,' Brodie said, 'I reckon our only hope is to use his reticence to our advantage.'

He slipped an arm beneath Genevieve's waist. Then, despite her protestations, he lifted her from the ground and hoisted her over his left shoulder.

He needed to use one arm to keep her steady with her head resting against his back and her legs clutched to his chest, but he could swing his gun arm freely.

Kyle nodded approvingly and so they both turned to the door while waiting for the best moment to make their move.

The flames had now reached the top of their side of the doorway and for the first time the heat made Brodie mop at his face. The smoke clawed at his throat confirming that they couldn't delay for long.

Kyle tapped his chest before pointing to his right and then signalled that Brodie should go in the opposite direction. This would take Kyle towards the last place they'd seen the devil's marshal, but as he was looking after Genevieve, Brodie nodded.

Kyle raised four fingers and then lowered a finger at a time. He was down to the last finger when something flickered in the firelight and then a mask came fluttering down to land in the middle of the doorway.

'At least that means we'll find out the truth,' Kyle said with grim humour. Then he lowered the finger.

With his head down he ran for the position where the devil's marshal must have been standing when he'd thrown the mask. Brodie followed Kyle's instructions by going to the other side of the doorway where he didn't dare pause in case the flames caught Genevieve.

He suffered a brief moment when he thought the intense heat would force him to turn back, but then his momentum took him outside into the cooler air. He swung round to look in the same direction as Kyle had gone, but their target wasn't there.

The four warehouses were all ablaze, bathing the site in brilliant light. He and Kyle edged out into the middle to put as much distance as possible between them and the flames.

For several minutes they glanced around nervously, but when the devil's marshal failed to appear, they bunched up to discuss tactics.

The fire illuminated the ground for two hundred yards behind them, but if they went in that direction they would be moving away from town and so Brodie nodded in the opposite direction.

'We head straight on,' he said.

Kyle grunted his agreement before he set off. Brodie walked ten paces behind him while looking sideways in case the killer had taken refuge on the rise.

Kyle had reached a point where he could see between the warehouses when he came to a sudden halt. He turned at the hip, his gun swinging round to pick out a target that Brodie couldn't see.

Then Kyle's mouth fell open in surprise and he took longer to aim than Brodie expected, giving his unseen opponent enough time to fire.

As the gunshot echoed around the site, Kyle dropped to his knees, his gun falling from his grasp and a hand rising to clutch his upper chest.

In a quick decision, Brodie rolled Genevieve from his shoulder and laid her down as gently as he could before he hurried on to Kyle. When Genevieve could see what had concerned him, she squealed with anguish, a sound that made Kyle raise his head to look at her.

Blood was seeping through his fingers, the liquid gleaming in the firelight, but he smiled. Then he keeled over on to his side.

Brodie remained alert, his gun trained on the space that was opening up between the warehouses, but he saw nobody there and even when he could see both walls, the devil's marshal wasn't visible.

While looking around for him, he knelt beside Kyle and turned him over on to his back.

'Tonight belonged to me and Genevieve,' Kyle said with his eyes closing, 'didn't it?'

'It did,' Brodie said. 'Everyone will remember seeing you two dancing together.'

'I waited for her and she chose me. Nobody could ask for anything more, could they?'

Brodie had now looked in all directions and he'd not seen any sign of the devil's marshal.

'They couldn't,' he said using the most calming tone he could manage. 'Rest now. I'll deal with him and then I'll get you back to town.'

Kyle mustered a barely perceptible shake of the head.

'Forget me. I was finished from the moment I dug up Derrick's grave. Just get her to safety.'

'If I'm to save her, it'd help to know what I'm up against.'

'They killed Derrick Shelby,' Kyle murmured, his voice fading, 'and they did it well. That's because they knew what to do.'

'Who is he?' Brodie urged.

'I forgot.' Kyle's voice had faded to a whisper and he appeared to be rambling to himself. 'We all forgot. But he didn't.'

Brodie waited, but when Kyle said no more, he shook his shoulder. That made Kyle's head roll to the side and his weak breath rustled the dust beyond his lips. The dust didn't move again.

Brodie patted his side and then got to his feet. He turned full circle without seeing Kyle's killer.

With him standing in the central point of the warehouses and flames on all sides, he reckoned the devil's marshal couldn't remain hidden for long.

Genevieve must have reached the same conclusion, as she tore her gaze away from looking at Kyle's body and then folded herself double before struggling up to a sitting position. She looked away from Brodie at the back end of the depot.

With one direction covered, Brodie turned to face in the opposite direction, ensuring that if the devil's marshal appeared between the warehouses or at the front end of the depot, he'd see him.

A minute passed and then another. Brodie figured that as he could see for some distance beyond the depot, the devil's marshal was unlikely to have fled, but his opponent's patience was likely to win the day.

The flames had now taken hold of the warehouse roofs sending flames shooting fifty feet into the air. The heat was drying the sweat on his brow.

He figured that by the time the warehouses were entirely alight, even in this central point, the depot would be a hellish inferno.

'They forgot you,' Brodie shouted, accepting that to get out of there alive he needed to make the devil's marshal show himself, 'and they sent you to hell. You returned and yet you're still in hell.'

He waited for a reply he doubted would come before he continued with the taunts.

'I don't know who you are, so you'll have to come out and tell me.'

He tried further taunts, but his voice

didn't sound as if it were loud enough to carry over the crackling flames.

Then, his skin starting to feel as if it were being baked, his throat dried up and his voice became hoarse. Walking steadily, he backed away to join Genevieve.

'We have to go,' Genevieve said simply.

Brodie nodded and then dropped to one knee to hoist her as efficiently as he could up on to a shoulder, his quick motion making her screech. He turned around, but then backed away for a pace when he saw that he'd misunderstood the reason for her distress.

She had been trying to warn him that the devil's marshal had returned.

The man stood beyond the front end of the depot, picking a spot between two warehouses so that he and Brodie could face each other. He had drawn his gun, but he held it low and he had tipped back his hat so that Brodie could see his face.

The man was about Brodie's age, but

the flames made his features appear haggard and the red light made the ridged scar tissue on his neck and around the mouth stand out. Brodie had never seen his face before and he doubted he'd met him before the scarring.

'Did you see his face?' he whispered to Genevieve.

'Only for a moment,' she said, 'and I've no idea who he is.'

'I gather you can't talk,' Brodie shouted, 'but I also know that before you take a life, you want to be remembered. How are you going to make that happen now?'

By way of an answer, the devil's marshal started walking towards him. The warehouses to either side were burning savagely and the fire created solid walls of flame that would bake a man to a crisp if he came within ten feet of them.

The devil's marshal walked down the centre, but that was still only thirty feet from the flames, a distance only a man who was familiar with pain could tolerate.

In response, Brodie settled his stance so that he could raise his gun quickly despite Genevieve's weight on his shoulder.

'When this place burns to the ground,' Brodie called, 'people will soon forget what happened here, and I reckon you'll be pleased to see the depot destroyed, too.'

His comment made the man stop beside Kyle's body. He was close enough for Brodie to see his eyes and they reflected light that was tinged with red.

'They killed Marshal Derrick Shelby and now you've killed them,' Brodie said, recalling Kyle's last words. 'They knew what to do and that's because . . . that's because they'd done it before, to someone else.'

The man nodded, forcing Brodie to think quickly. On his shoulder, Genevieve shifted position, presumably in concern about his revelation, but he persisted.

'They cut out your tongue and buried you alive, but you escaped from that terrible death. The next time, they ensured Derrick didn't survive. You didn't kill them in revenge for what they did to Derrick, but for what they did to you. Now you've moved on to take revenge against this woman, me, and even the whole town, but we don't remember you because we had nothing to do with what happened. That's wrong.'

Brodie had no hope that the devil's marshal would listen to his plea for clemency, but to his surprise, the man considered him with a gaze that flickered with uncertainty before he backed away for a pace.

Then he turned to face the fire raging in the warehouse ahead of him. He set off, walking steadily towards the flames.

When Brodie saw what he intended to do, he broke into a stumbling run. Encumbered with Genevieve on his shoulder, he couldn't hope to reach the man in time and, after only a few paces, the heat made his eyes water and the hot air made him gasp.

Through his blurred vision, he saw the devil's marshal turn back to him. He must have misinterpreted his actions as he snapped up his gun arm.

On the run, Brodie reacted instantly and two gunshots rang out as they both fired.

Trapped on all sides by the raging heat and the dazzling light, both men's aim was poor. So Brodie ran on.

Every pace took him closer to the inferno, making his skin tighten and making Genevieve murmur in distress. He fired again and then shook his head hoping to clear his vision, the action making him stumble to one knee.

In a moment of clarity, he saw the devil's marshal standing in harsh relief before a swirling wall of flame. He had crouched over clutching a blooded side, but he'd also aimed at Brodie's head and from ten feet away he couldn't miss him.

Without much hope Brodie snapped

his gun arm up, but the burning hell before him was too bright to look at directly and he struggled to take aim. He fired with his gaze averted.

Long moments passed in which the end he expected didn't overcome him. Then, in a shocking moment, understanding hit him and he realized why he'd been spared.

The inferno had filled his vision because it was getting closer; the building behind the devil's marshal was collapsing.

Brodie hunched over while twisting away, catching one last sight of the devil's marshal standing poised with his gun thrust out as the burning building fell forward to consume him. Then he could only lie down with his back turned, protecting Genevieve while praying that the fire didn't take them too.

Crashes sounded and a burst of heat that made him screech tore across his back. He also thought he heard Genevieve scream, but the cacophony of noise stole the sound away.

His calf throbbed with a sharp, hot pain, making him draw the leg away. When he looked down, he saw that the top of a burning wall had landed five feet away from him, but that was the nearest part of the fallen warehouse.

He couldn't see the devil's marshal.

He shook Genevieve's shoulder. She was wide-eyed and murmuring with concern and so this time he put his hands beneath her and clutched her to his chest.

With her arms wrapped around his neck, he walked away from the inferno, fixing his gaze on a point where there were no flames and ignoring all distractions.

Behind him more crashes sounded as walls and then whole buildings collapsed, but he kept on walking out of the depot and then across open land. Only when they were a hundred yards beyond the fire did Brodie relent and place Genevieve on the ground.

They lay on their sides enjoying the

cool air and watching the flames claim the old depot until approaching movement made him sit up. He saw that the townsfolk had returned, but thankfully, they looked at them only with concern.

Someone produced a knife and in short order several men combined forces to free Genevieve.

When the ropes fell away, she rolled on to her back. She took several minutes to massage the cramps from her limbs during which time the rest of the warehouses crashed to the ground.

When the last building settled down into a heap of firewood, Genevieve still looked shocked after hearing details of her husband's demise, so Brodie took her hand. He left the townsfolk to watch the final death throes of the depot while he led her back to town.

He moved quickly, fearful of what he'd find when he arrived, but to his relief, no siege of the law office of the kind he'd seen on his first night here was developing. In fact, nobody was on the main drag as everyone's interest was centred on the burning buildings.

With Genevieve at his side, he headed into the law office, hoping that the crisis was now over, but he quickly came to a halt and bade her stay back. Erskine was lying sprawled over his desk.

He shook him, but he couldn't rouse him, although the deputy did murmur groggily. Brodie couldn't find any obvious wounds and so he hurried to the jailhouse.

Phineas Moon's cell door was swinging open; Phineas had gone. Nobody else was there.

'I'll check in the hotel,' Genevieve said when he returned to the law office. 'Lucinda and Chauncey have probably taken refuge there.'

Brodie nodded and bade her be careful, but when she'd left, Erskine started snoring loudly, putting Brodie in mind of a similar occasion recently when he'd knocked out Lucinda's guards with a sleeping draught.

'Except,' he said to himself, 'I've got a feeling they won't be there.'

15

In the days that followed the burning down of the depot, the town gradually returned to normality. Nobody else was kidnapped, but of the escaped Phineas Moon and the missing Chauncey and Lucinda there was no sign.

Even the body of the devil's marshal couldn't be found, although ash was all that remained of the warehouses.

Brodie devoted his time to writing up reports and making the case for Lucinda's innocence. When he sounded out Erskine with his version of events, the deputy accepted his report with more enthusiasm than he'd shown so far.

With Erskine's acquiescence suggesting he should be able to convince a judge that the devil's marshal had killed Archibald Harper and the others, Brodie turned his thoughts to resolving the other mysteries.

Six days after rescuing Genevieve, he finally worked out what had happened to Phineas Moon.

He was still leaning back in his chair and basking in the glory of piecing together the clues when Genevieve came to see him for the first time since Kyle's funeral.

'I've found out who the devil's marshal was,' she said. She used a sombre tone, although Brodie noted that she hadn't reverted to black clothing.

'I'm impressed.' He bade her to sit at Erskine's desk. 'I've spent the last week asking everyone in town and nobody has any idea who he could be, and that includes men who have lived here since the early days.'

'That doesn't surprise me. He was Gideon Gale.'

Brodie shrugged. 'The name means nothing to me.'

'I was looking through Derrick's old letters and I found the one that invited him to become Hamilton's new town marshal. The previous lawman had arrived in town and booked into my hotel, but he'd failed to survive for long enough to see his first sundown.'

She raised an eyebrow, inviting Brodie to piece together the remainder of the story.

'Gideon Gale was a lawman who asked too many questions of the wrong people, too quickly,' he ventured. When she nodded he spoke with greater confidence. 'He was taken prisoner and buried alive, except he escaped. He licked his wounds and then returned to take revenge only to find he wasn't the only lawman to suffer his fate and worse, everyone had forgotten him.'

'That's what happened, but not everyone has forgotten him. We can now make sure he'll be remembered.'

Brodie nodded. 'Like your husband, he was the only one with the guts to confront the guilty, and he suffered the consequences. With more support he'd have made this town a better place.'

'He would have and hopefully, with that mystery resolved, you'll now have the time to find your sister.'

'I don't need to. She's with Chauncey and, for all his faults, he clearly cares for her and he'll keep her safe no matter what Phineas plans to do next.' He noted that Genevieve looked confused and so he explained what he'd learnt from the law office records. 'Phineas Moon was caught eleven times and he escaped eleven times.'

Brodie laughed making Genevieve frown.

'What's so amusing about that?'

'Because every time he was captured, he was brought in by a man matching Chauncey's description. As soon as that bounty hunter got his bounty, Phineas escaped, and I reckon it's obvious who helped him.'

Brodie didn't add that he presumed Chauncey had used him as, when Chauncey had suggested he drug the guards to free his sister, he'd already secreted a key to Phineas. Instead, he concentrated on the more important point that with Chauncey repeatedly catching the same man, he'd never beat his own tally of successful manhunts.

Genevieve shrugged. 'Chauncey can't keep carrying out that ruse for ever.'

'I know. Things change, and I reckon my sister will change him for the better.'

'I reckon she will, too.' Genevieve got up from the desk. With a pensive expression, she headed to the door where she turned back to him and sighed. 'I cared for Kyle, although perhaps not as much as he cared for me.'

'I understand.'

'With the last dance going so well, at least for a while, I reckon I'll postpone my decision about leaving until after I've held another one.' She offered a smile. 'Will you come?'

'I'd like another chance to show you how good a dancer I am.' He returned the smile. 'But only if I can have the first dance.'

'You can.' She opened the door. 'And the last one, too.'

THE END

We do hope that you have enjoyed reading this large print book.

Did you know that all of our titles are available for purchase?

We publish a wide range of high quality large print books including:
Romances, Mysteries, Classics
General Fiction
Non Fiction and Westerns

Special interest titles available in large print are:
The Little Oxford Dictionary
Music Book, Song Book
Hymn Book, Service Book

Also available from us courtesy of Oxford University Press:
Young Readers' Dictionary
(large print edition)
Young Readers' Thesaurus
(large print edition)

For further information or a free brochure, please contact us at:
Ulverscroft Large Print Books Ltd.,
The Green, Bradgate Road, Anstey,
Leicester, LE7 7FU, England.
Tel: (00 44) **0116 236 4325**
Fax: (00 44) **0116 234 0205**

POWDER RIVER

Jack Edwardes

As the State Governor's lawmen spread throughout Wyoming, the days of the bounty hunter are coming to a close. For hired gun Brad Thornton, this spells the end of an era. The men in badges aren't yet everywhere, though, and rancher Moreton Frewen needs immediate action: rustlers are stealing his stock, and Thornton is just the man to make the culprits pay. But these are no run-of-the-mill cattle thieves. The Morgan gang are ruthless killers, prepared to turn their hands to anything from bank robbery to murder . . .

THE HONOUR OF THE BADGE

Scott Connor

US Marshal Stewart Montague was a respected mentor to young Deputy Lincoln Hawk, guiding his first steps as a lawman and impressing upon him the importance of the honour of the badge. Twenty years later, the pair are pursuing a gang of bandits when Montague goes missing, presumed murdered. For six months, Hawk continues the mission alone, without success. But when he stumbles into the gang's hideout, there is a great shock in store. Seems his old companion isn't six feet under after all . . .

RETURN OF THE BANDIT

Roy Patterson

Villainous bounty hunter Hume Crawford is well-known for his brutal slayings: he will do anything to get his hands on those he seeks. Out to find and kill the legendary bandit Zococa, despite reports of the good-natured rogue's death, Crawford proceeds to shoot his way across the Mexican border. But he has attracted the attention of Marshal Hal Gunn and his deputy Toby Jones. As Crawford follows Zococa's trail, there are two Texas star riders on his . . .

THE PHANTOM STRIKES

Walt Keene

The desert terrain was once haunted by the Phantom — a blanched man on a pale-grey horse, who struck in the night and killed without mercy. Wild Bill Hickock shot the legend down once — and twenty years later, when the Phantom's son took up the torch, he did so again . . . With both culprits dead, Hickock and his compadres are satisfied they have laid the ghost to rest. But when a mortally wounded man gasps that the spirit has returned, they must take up arms once more — against the Phantom's second son . . .